Dea

I've some brilliant news. Yes, you've guessed it – I've finally found our flat! The ck facs – cooking facilities – are just one electric ring, but as we're going to get healthy and only cook Ryvita from now on, who cares? OUR OWN PLACE AT LAST!

I'm sorry I didn't share the good news with you straightaway on the phone tonight but I don't have a shred of privacy in this dungeon and I don't dare let Mum and Dad know where I'm going. They're bound to tell me they won't let me do it, and I can't risk that – not after everything I've been through. So I've got no choice. I'm going to have to scarper, do a moonlit flit, take French Leave.

LiveWiRE

from The Women's Press

Eileen Fairweather is an award-winning freelance journalist and author. She has contributed to numerous national newspapers and magazines, television documentaries and radio, and enjoys writing humorous fiction as a contrast from journalism.

In 1993 she won a British Press Award for her investigative reporting of child abuse. She is also a winner of the *Evening Standard* Catherine Pakenham Award for women journalists. She is the author of *French Letters: The Life and Loves of Miss Maxine Harrison* (Livewire, 1987), and co-author of *Only the Rivers Run Free: Northern Ireland, the Women's War.*

Eileen Fairweather was raised in London and has a daughter.

French Leave

Maxine Harrison Moves Out!

Eileen Fairweather

Livewire

For my daughter Katarina,
so bright and brave

Almost at the end of the Easter holidays
On a coach
On a motorway
Taking me away from
My Best Friend

Ms Jean Oglethorpe
The Whippet's Welcome
Furnace Street
Ashton-under-Lyne
Lancashire
The Far North

Dearest Jean,

The wrinklie in the seat next to me has finally stopped yabbering and started to snore, so I'm writing to say THANK YOU for the best holiday in my life.

Admittedly it's the *only* holiday in my life, given I'm a deprived child. But tonight, as the coach hurtles through the Northern rain back to London, I feel like an exotic explorer. Most holiday-makers have never even *heard* of Ashton-under-Lyne.

Actually, I'm writing to stop myself feeling scared. When I get back, Mum and Dad will have made their Big Decision about my future. Can you keep a secret? If they make the wrong one, I am going to LEAVE HOME! I'm sure it's legal to scarper at 16 – you can learn to drive and bonk then, and they're far more technical.

I don't even want to think about that now (leaving home I mean!) so I'm concentrating on Positive Thoughts instead. Won't Muck Mouth Michelle be sick

1

as a pig at school next week when I tell her where I've been?

She always said you'd forget me after you moved Oop North. So isn't it great that after fifteen months apart we're still best mates? I'm not even jealous of that Sharon girl. You need someone at your new school to hang round with – even if she is a bit slow. I only point that out because she laughed at me for running through the daffodils reciting, 'I wandered lonely as a cloud'. Why didn't you join in? That's our Easter *tradition*.

At least I don't think Wordsworth's a band.

Whatever Sharon says, I'm not a snotty Southerner. Truly, I'm impressed by your family's rediscovery of its Northern roots. Your dad's made a mint converting the Queen's Arms into the Whippet's Welcome, and your new Coronation Street accent is almost convincing. OK, I nearly threw up when your 'mam' told me Black Pudding is made from dried pig's blood, but her Lancashire Hot Pot is fab.

I've just one worry, which I hope you won't think is racist. Has the softer water up North softened your brain? Once upon a time, Jean, you too had *ambitions*! All right, they were daft ones – whoever heard of a pop star with next to no nose? But at least you dreamed. Now you're talking about quitting school after this term's exams.

Get real, Jean! You're in the top stream and about to pull off a bundle of GCSEs. We've slaved five years for this. Stick it out for another couple of years, take your A levels, and we could get to UNIVERSITY. Yes, you and me – who Muck Mouth once labelled the 'tatty working-class thickies' of Haringey Girls.

I don't know how to break this to you but recently I've realised that, despite my tragic family background and addiction to *Neighbours*, I am an intellectual at heart.

2

I thought secretly you were too. So why throw your life away pulling pints in the family pub?

You *know* my parents are thinking of forcing me out to work. If I can say *you're* staying on at school, they might just stop droning on that education's 'not for the likes of us'. I'm too young to become a child labourer.

I don't want to make you feel responsible, Jean, but if you drop out you'll be throwing away my life too.

Thanks again for the great holiday, it really cheered me up.

I'll let you know asap whether I've got any future.

Your grateful friend,

Maxine

The Horrid Harrison Household
96 Sheraton Road
Terminally Boring Hornsey
London N8

Friday

Dear Jean,

I don't want you worrying unnecessarily so I am writing to reassure you about my future.

I haven't got one.

My disgusting parents broke the news last night with their usual sensitivity.

'Well, Maxie,' Dad said the minute I got in, 'You can forget about becoming an actress or a Do Gooder.' (What

3

he calls social workers.) 'Your mother and me have been doing our sums — and they just don't add up.'

Just because he's unemployed and his benefit's been cut, they reckon they can't afford to keep me on at school. They're so mean.

Apparently, I should think myself lucky because Marks and Spencer's have invited me in for an interview. Don't die of excitement, Jean, but I may have a full-time job in lingerie this summer, and Mum and Dad think they might keep me on after that. Dad even tried to turn the death of my dreams into a joke.

'Just think, love,' he said, winking, 'They'll never invent a machine capable of measuring a woman's bosom, so you'll have a job for life!'

Brain damage within two years more like! Just how excited can you get about selling a 34D and matching knickers? Maybe I could if I were more like my sister Sue. But despite the same impoverished gene pool, I'm not.

And no, M & D were not impressed by my new supercool short spiky hairstyle. In fact Dad said I looked like a toilet brush. Mum, who'd been making sympathetic noises up to then and looking anxious, even had the nerve to laugh.

The sad thing is, Dad's right. Later, after I'd screamed at them for ruining my life, I inspected my hair and I look *awful*. Why did I let you talk me into that backstreet butcher of a hairdresser? Thank God my hair grows fast. And, as soon as it does, I'm going to leave home, work all day and save up to get my A Levels.

Yes, Jean, I've made up my mind. I HATE exams and I LOATHE revision, but I am NOT going to end up like my sickening sister. Just 17 and already she's thrown in the towel.

'Guess what Derek bought me!' Sue trilled, waltzing

into our bedroom and completely ignoring my swollen
eyes.

Another engagement ring? I asked. A set of wheels?
A suspender belt with tinsel straps? No, the cause of all
this excitement was a *potato masher*.

'For my bottom drawer,' she cooed.

'Open it quick,' I felt like saying, 'I need to throw up.'

Maybe I'm just jealous. A potato masher might not be
my idea of passion – and deathly Derek certainly isn't.
But at least Sue's found a man who wants to marry her.
Frankie's such a slow mover I'll be drawing my pension
before he asks me to mash his lumps. Not that I approve
of marriage, but I could do with a little romance.

What am I going to do about *that* too? I'm too young
to give up on passion. Especially since I've never experi-
enced any.

It could get pretty lonely in a bed-sit, with a frigid
boyfriend and a best friend 203 miles away.

The point is, Jean, I need to ask a small favour.

When I move out, will you come too?

Love,

Maxine

Sunday night
Last night of Freedom
Betrayed in Hornsey

Et tu Jean. How *could* you? I thought you were ringing
me up tonight to wish me luck for tomorrow – God
knows I need it. Or to say you wanted to leave home

5

too. Instead, all I get is a lecture about how you're sure my parents will come round in the end and that leaving home is a BIG DECISION.

I know *that*. And I've already decided. As I told you on the phone *and* in my last letter, it's A Levels or Bust. And no of course I'm not moving out *immediately*. Even *my* hair doesn't grow *that* fast. I won't begin to look presentable until the summer. Besides, we've got our exams first – or have you forgotten?

Honestly, Jean, I thought you at least would have more confidence in me. And then you accuse me of guilt-tripping you? I'm only concerned about your future. At least I *try* to be positive.

Still, I'm sorry I slammed the phone down. I really did have to run to get ready for school tomorrow. And I'm sorry I yelled at you. I'd just spent a horrid weekend ignoring my parents, just to make sure they got the message.

Anyway, it looks like I'll have to get used to facing life on my own from now on. Even Frankie hasn't been round.

Wishing you a pleasant start to your last term,

Maxine Harrison

First day back at Haringey Girls
say no more . . .

Dear Jean,

It's 2.05 pm and my first free period for revision. But after all this trauma, I feel completely at a loss. I can't work out where to start, what to prioritise, or which textbook to open. So instead I'm stuffing my face with Smarties on the sly.

Please excuse my last letter, Jean. I've thought it over and maybe you were just concerned about me after all. I know I care what happens to you. That's what being friends is all about, isn't it? Let's make it up. I'll forgive your slip in judgement if you'll forgive mine. I guess that's what Mum means when she sighs and says, 'I know you *mean* well, Maxine.'

This morning Bat-Face gave us a stern lecture about how we Young Ladies facing exams just need Back Bone. No we don't. We need CHOCOLATE, preferably mainlined. And supportive families. But does she care? Does she hell.

At break time I bravely broke it to her that I might be forced to leave Haringey Girls to get a job. I was hoping she'd ask me to sit down but she barely looked up from her desk.

'Really, Maxine? Well, I'm sure the school's loss will be the working world's gain.'

I sniffed miserably, but she wasn't impressed.

'You know the routine,' she sighed. 'You should discuss this with one of the teachers responsible for Careers, not me.'

Hard-faced humiliating cow – as if I'd want to bare my soul a second time round.

Yeah, I know, more fool me for confiding in Bat-Face. But I'd lain awake all night thinking about your suggestion that I tell somebody in authority about my dilemma. She was the first one I came across. How could I have forgotten she thinks girls on free school dinners Lower The Tone of the school?

I know I should pull myself together. But it's easier

7

said than done. So here I am writing to you under cover of my atlas. You and Smarties are the only things I can depend on . . .

Please let's make it up.

Your anxious pal,

Max

Monday
10.15 pm

Dearest Jean,

You've just hung up on me, and I feel so much better. I'm so glad you were feeling dreadful about our argument too. Of course I understand that the call had to be quick. I know it's hard to get to the phone while your dad's not looking – I just hadn't realised he's started getting an itemised bill. Talk about sneaky as well as stingy.

I really missed you today. By now I should be used to my best friend's desertion. (Only kidding!) It's just that whenever a new term starts and I wearily slink back in through those gates, I still wish you were slinking in beside me.

You remember what the first day back is like – everyone competing over who's been doing what, and to who.

Muck Mouth Michelle has obviously been doing that prat Keith Edwards. Now she's flashing his engagement ring.

Poor Rosie. She *hates* Keith. You remember how he had that one snogging session with her, then told all of Hornsey Boys he'd gone the whole way?

Muck Mouth was the first to call Rosie a slag, but this lunch-time in the canteen she was loudly boasting that Keith treats *her* like a 'real lady'. Rosie got up to go for her but a couple of us pulled her down. Good old Grace, our normally clean-mouthed Baptist, said, 'Girl, you got to turn the other cheek. The Lord punishes sinners. That's why he put that bum-ugly bitch and sexist nerd together.'

I hope you don't mind me hanging round with Rosie. It's a bit like you and Sharon. No one could take *your* place. I just need someone at school who's on the same wave-length. Rosie agrees with me that girls should go for it — careers, travel, dreams.

Counting Muck Mouth, there are now three girls in Year 10 who have fiancés. I'm so glad I believe in staying single. If I didn't, I might feel left out.

I thought everyone would be impressed by my fort-night inspecting your new home in the Far North. I lied and said your horrible brother Bob the Dog was now dead good looking and, despite the fact that Ashton-under-Lyne makes Coronation Street seem posh, I made it sound quite glamorous. But then Michelle — she's been to Majorca *again*! — spoiled it all.

'My Keith wouldn't let me go away for more than a week,' she preened, 'He'd miss me too much.'

Then she smirked, 'How *is* your Frankie, Max? Seen him yet?'

Actually, I *still* haven't. Sue caught me nicking her styling gel this morning and had the cheek to nick it back before I was finished. So I was left with half my hair stiff and spiky and the other half as flat as a squashed hedgehog. That of course is when Frankie called round to walk me to school. I had to make Mum pretend I'd already left.

I'd begged her to buy me some more gel — I got through that whole Body Shop pot in three days! But she gave me GBH of the earhole about how many bed-pans she has to empty just to buy the cheapo supermarket mousse.

'Yeah, the kind that destroys the ozone layer!' I snapped.

'The kind we can AFFORD,' she said. The soulless polluter.

Money, money, money. That's all my dead-head family care about since Dad went on the sick.

'No wonder you've signed my life away to Marks,' I said. 'You wouldn't know a finer feeling if it hit you in the face.'

Dad looked ready to hit me in mine when I dropped my bombshell. I know it's supposed to be a secret, but the strain was too much. So I told them I was planning to Leave Home. The effect was really dramatic. Dad said, 'Good — then you'll find out what everything costs.' Mum just said, 'Don't be daft,' and went back to her ironing.

They don't even care. Face it, I'm as good as abandoned already. Please, please write back soon. I really am glad your first day back was better than mine.

Your best friend,

Max

PS   I don't want to put pressure on you, but why haven't you decided yet to move in with me? Tonight you didn't even mention my exciting offer before hanging up.

You're always saying I'm selfish, Jean, but honestly it's your welfare I'm thinking of. Why put up with Bob the Dog when you could be spending time with me? I know you pretend to be proud of your family's Northern roots, which is really brave of you. But it's only your mum and Nan, poor things, that were Ashton born and bred. It's time for you to get back to *your* birthplace – in the Sophisticated South.

96 Sheraton Slums
Hornsey

April 17th

Dear Jean

OK, OK, I'm *sorry*! I was only joking, I didn't really mean to be rude about Ashton-under-Slime. If I were a sensitive person, you calling me a Southern Racist would really hurt.

Fortunately one of the few advantages of being disadvantaged is that you grow a thick skin. Since Dad gave up the buses – or rather the buses gave up him – mine's grown so thick I could hire myself out as a trampoline. Otherwise, I'd die of shame every time Michelle refers to those 'work-shy scroungers' just to get at me.

All right, you're right, maybe I AM jealous of you. Your dad's turned a tatty pub into a trendy wine bar, and made enough dosh to drape at least twenty gold chains around his neck. All my dad's draped in is nervous eczema.

But let's get one thing clear. I am NOT jealous of your new accent. I am sincerely glad, Jean, that the North is finally undergoing a revival, and sure it's cool nowadays to talk like a Scouse or a Geordie. I agree you haven't a chance in hell of fronting a youth programme on TV if you don't. But you're telling me it's *sexy* now to sound like a character from *Coronation Street*? Jean – *please!* Trendy – maybe. Seductive – *never.*

And about those new down-to-earth Northern values you've recently acquired. Do *they* explain why you don't want to be a singer anymore, a star?

Maybe our dreams when we were younger *were* silly. But when you threw out those tapes of us singing together and threw yourself into the Red Cross, I thought you'd at least end up becoming a doctor. Now you, Ms Top of the Class, are saying that maybe you want to be a nurse??!!

Oh Jean!

I'm sorry – I'm a cow. I just feel so *alone* with this ambition thing. My family's got such a downer on it. They won't let *themselves* have hopes, never mind me.

I really looked up to Dad when he was a bus conductor and shop steward, even if I did sometimes pretend he was the boss of London Transport. But then its real boss pushed through his horrid 'One Man Bus' scheme and Dad bottled out of driving because he couldn't handle the 'stress'. Since then, he's turned into a real wimp.

I keep telling him to retrain but he says he's too old. He's so *negative*! He's not even grateful to Mum for taking on her hospital job on top of her shifts at Bert's greasy spoon.

'We wouldn't *have* a mortgage to worry about,' he's always saying, 'if *she* hadn't made us buy this place.'

As an 'old style' socialist he says he doesn't hold with

council house sales. You'd better believe the 'old style' bit – he isn't half prejudiced. Tonight Mum came home all excited because this male nurse told her she was a 'natural' and should train to be a proper nurse herself. Dad kiboshed that straightaway.

'What would *he* know?' he snorted. 'He's just some nancy in a frock.'

I think he's scared Mum might want to follow my example and become a Career Woman too. Poor Mum. I know I hate her at the moment but she looked so squashed.

Yes, I know I was snotty a minute ago about you becoming a nurse, but that's *different*. You can do algebra equations in your head, remember chemical formulae without looking them up, and are so effortlessly clever you make me sick.

Face it, Jean, you've a zillion advantages. I haven't even got much of a home life compared to you. Your parents love you for *who you are*. Maybe that's why they're so laid-back about whether you stay on at school or not.

I'm sorry I poked fun at Lancs. To tell the truth, it's only because it has you and I don't. In other words, *I miss you.*

You're always saying that Northerners are more genu-ine and say what they mean. Did you mean it when you said I'm a wally?

I note that you *still* haven't replied to my brilliant suggestion that we live together.

Please reconsider. I wasn't joking about *that* bit.

You might even find that living with a wally is quite fun really.

I'll await your reply in the earliest post. Now, I've got to run. Yes, Frankie's back in my life – or soon will be.

13

I've only got an hour and a half to get ready. It's mega date time!

Yours,

Max

Bonanza Flat Share Competition Ltd
Hornsey

Friday

Dear Ms Jean Oglethorpe,

CONGRATULATIONS! You have been personally hand-picked by our computer to join three million other lucky entrants in our Prize Draw. First Prize: Becoming Ms Maxine Harrison's Flatemate!

Seriously, Jean, I'm thrilled you're finally 'thinking about' living with me. But why do you sound so nervous? Most people would jump at the chance I'm offering you. It's not *really* such a 'big step'. I know you're proud of being Sensible, but if you spend your whole life sitting on the fence you'll end up with splinters.

What exactly are you worrying about? You *won't* have to 'leave Patch'. The British are a nation of animal lovers, remember. We're bound to find a landlady somewhere who'd love to house an incontinent dog.

Be positive — think of the advantages! You won't have to hide my letters from your brother any more — or put up with his filthy innuendos. Of course he can't understand our friendship or us wanting to 'live together'. *His* closest 'relationship' is with a part of his own body!

14

You wouldn't even have to sacrifice your Born Again Northerner accent – you could keep it up by watching *Coronation Street*. Other nights, we could go out or do each other's hair. I don't mean to hurt your feelings, Jean, but you're right: you really *do* need a good friend's daily help in straightening out those curls.

Once we've got you looking presentable, we could even get dead posh and invite friends Round For Dinner. That's what Amanda and Nathan next door do while we plebby Harrisons are eating our tea.

Talking of Amanda, guess what? When I was baby-sitting her snotty kids last night and going through her drawers, I discovered she's starting something right up my alley. A Youth Drama Group!

There was a notice in her college newsletter advertising the auditions. Plus all these private notes to herself about wanting to illuminate the Plight of Alienated Youth. I couldn't understand most of it, but I know she's very keen on illuminating things, seeing as she's a lecturer in Cultural and Communication Studies.

So when she and Nathan got back, I mentioned, very natural like, that I'd been feeling very deprived lately. Of course I couldn't let on that I'd been snooping, so I just casually worked the chat round to Cultural Things. I said how bad the soaps were getting (well, she hates them) and how much classier they'd be if I were in them.

'But of course,' I said pitifully, 'I'll never get a chance to act. Because my dad's so mean – I mean, poor – he thinks my starring role in life should be behind a shop counter.'

Amanda looked a bit guilty then, and Nathan fiddled with one of his badges. 'Teachers Against Teaching' or

15

something. Finally, he said, 'Go on, Ammie, why not let her join in?'

So Amanda told me about the group and got me to write down all the details about the audition. I sounded ever so grateful, even though I'd already put 'May 10th, 7 pm, Comfortable Clothes' in my diary.

'It's going to be a very *alternative* company, though,' she said, like she was warning me about something. I can't think why, I know what 'alternative' means. I've already worked out something dead alternative for the audition. I'm going to recite our poem, 'I wandered lonely as a cloud'. The alternative bit will be me dressing up as a homeless daffodil (yellow clothes, cardboard box).

Don't laugh. Even though I'm hitting the Smarties hard in the run-up to the GCSEs, I've kept my weight down so I'm relatively willowy. No, I'm not on a sweets-followed-by-starvation diet; I just do a hundred neurotic sit-ups every time I eat.

Not that anyone here cares about my health. Dad yelled at me the other night for bouncing on the floor-boards and making the lights flicker. It was my head. Sit-ups are impossible with no one to hold your feet.

Honestly, Jean, it'll be such a relief to live with some-one who understands the importance of diet and exercise. I almost wish it were summer already – *despite* the GCSEs. I can't wait! I *knew* you'd come through.

Much love,

Max, your future flatmate

PS   In all the excitement, I nearly forgot! What do you think I should do about Frankie? He CANCELLED our mega date the other night . . . for *Deirdre*. No, my new rival's not tall, elegant and beautiful. She's tubby, greasy-skinned and fast. Don't ask me what he sees in her – I already know. She can do 80 miles an hour and I can't.

What chance do I have now he's finally got a motor-bike? No wonder I've hardly seen him. Apparently it's a big moment in a bloke's life, turning 17 and getting your 125 license. But that didn't stop me having a good rant at him.

Fancy calling a bike 'Deirdre' – how daft can you get? Frankie gave me his best blue-eyed look and said that Deirdre was a brave Irish warrior queen, and didn't that appeal to the feminist in me? As I'd already gone to the bother of shaving my legs, I told him to stick his Irish blarney. But how long do you think I should keep up my sulk?

Advice, please. SOON!

PPS   He's promised me a 'proper date' tomorrow, so I'll keep you posted.

Hornsey

April 20th
11.45 pm

Dear Jean,

I'm writing this straight after my 'proper date' with Frankie. Well, it was certainly proper – I haven't got a hair out of place, never mind a bra strap!

Don't get me wrong – I haven't turned into a complete sex maniac. I just wish I could get Frankie beyond Number Two. Also, that his idea of a Proper Date wasn't

17

The Three Brewers. There's a limit to how long you can make half a lager last. Mine's two hours, including the time it takes to chew through a packet of mints and worry about whether Mum will smell the booze on my breath. She only allows me near the place because I swear I stick to diet coke!

The worst thing was, Sue and Dead-End Derek pitched up within seconds of us arriving. I'd found us a nice dark corner, planning to work in a quick cuddle once Frankie had finished begging for forgiveness. But sweet sister Sue worked her way in instead. She's so diplomatic. If I'd had 'I want to be alone' tattooed on my forehead, she'd still have barged in.

It's all right for her and Derek — he's got his own flat. I bet they're at it every chance they get. I'm not stupid. I know she wouldn't hide them under the carpet if they really *were* vitamin pills.

God knows why she muscled in on what little privacy me and Frankie get. She just wanted to show off I suppose. Please don't have a heart attack from the excitement, Jean, but she and D have finally Named the Day.

Pathetically anaemic Sue's plumped for a wedding in early September, just so she can tan her bod all summer long. I ask you, Jean, how trivial can you *get*? Marriage is a sacred sacrament, a life-long commitment, but my sister plans hers around which month her skin's least grey. If I believed in marriage, I'd be quite disgusted. It'll serve her right if it ends in divorce.

I do hope I don't sound bitter. But the only reason I agreed to being gassed at close range by Derek's aftershave was his suggestion that we celebrate with champagne. Well, I'd never had it before.

I *still* haven't, Jean. The minute I said, 'Yes, please!'

Derek piped up, 'Right – coming to the bar to help me, Frankie?' I knew what that was really a code for and so did poor broke Frankie. Cough up, prove you're a man, pay half, or look tight-fisted.

What a cheek! That Derek with his fancy salesman's car is coining in God knows what just for hawking insurance. He *knows* that all Frankie's got while he's studying is his Saturday supermarket wages and odd-jobs money!

Poor Frankie turned bright red, and Sue's lip curled so much it looked like a pink crisp.

I did try to save Frankie's face. 'I've just remembered,' I said, 'I don't like spirits.'

But that made Sue snigger even more. 'Champagne's a *wine*, you silly girl.'

Well that was it. Frankie wasn't going to sit by and watch me be insulted. So he got up and left.

'I'll be back soon,' he said. 'Got to see a man about . . . about my bike.'

I thought that was a really dignified exit line. But when the Happy Couple finally settled down to *their* champagne, Sue acted like she was really sorry for me.

'Frankie doesn't make much of a fuss of you, does he?' she said, polishing her engagement ring against her jacket. 'Still, you two have only a very . . . *casual* thing, don't you?'

'No we don't,' I said. 'He's my steady boyfriend.'

Sue looked a bit sceptical so I threw in, 'Well, what else do you call a fella you see nearly every day?'

'Your next door neighbour?' she sneered.

I pointed out that the Maloneys actually live five doors down. But that just gave Sue the chance to preen about her 'adventurous' social life. God, you'd think she was about to make some exotic mixed race marriage, just cos Derek's from *Orpington*.

19

Fortunately, Frankie returned then and offered to buy a round. He told me later he'd skedaddled to borrow the money from Imelda. Now *she's* what I call a good sister. She wouldn't beat Frankie up for borrowing her dresses, the way Sue beats up me.

If Frankie were a girl, I mean.

Luckily, he didn't have to waste his money on those meanies because Mr and Mrs-to-be announced they wanted to go clubbing.

'So do I,' I said. 'But sororicide is against the law.' I *think* that's the Latin for killing your sister.

It's a good job Derek and Sue left school with only four GCSEs between them. They may have more money than Frankie and me, but at least we know when we're being insulted.

I tell a lie – tonight wasn't all awful. Frankie did give me a real smackeroonie of a kiss on the doorstep. Real let-my-tongue-lick-your-fillings stuff. But Mum soon put paid to that by going into her my-curtains-are-stuck routine.

It's horrible having a mum who's a voyeur. After five minutes of her fiddling with the nets, I didn't feel up to any more fiddling myself.

So here I am, tucked up in bed with my cocoa. All I've got to look forward to is Frankie's Surprise Present. He says he's only this broke because he's saving up for our first anniversary – that's the week after next!

Please send me something to cheer me up. How about your brother's body? Frankly, by now, even Bob the Dog's would do.

Yours in chastity,

Max

20

April 23rd

Dear Jean,

Thanks for your sensitive advice tonight about over-
coming Frankie's frigidity. You are quite right, what we
need is privacy. We're tragic, really. The Romeo and
Juliet of London N8 with nowhere to go.

Just be grateful, Jean, that your nose may have saved
you from this terrible fate. You know I think you're too
hard on yourself, and that your non-existent nose is quite
sweet really if you like that kind of thing. But what if
you're right and it *is* your nose that's kept you boyfriend-
less for the past four months, three weeks and two days?

If so, love your little snub nose, Jean, for saving you
from temptation. As I know from bitter experience,
having a boyfriend is all very well, but it's very frustrating
if you never get a second alone together.

Mum and Dad are *so* selfish. They're always in the
front room when me and Frankie want a snuggle on
the sofa. And now that Dad's out of work, he clutters
up the house all day as well as all night. If he really loved
me, he'd be respectably employed like other fathers. Then
I could be unrespectably employed while he's out.

Don't parents sicken you with their filthy minds? Yesterday, in desperation, I tried to get Frankie up to my
bedroom. But Mum planted herself like a Rottweiler at
the foot of the stairs.

'Where do you think you're going, Missy?' she hissed.

I was so scared I said the first thing that came into my
head.

'To play some CDs.'

'You haven't *got* any,' she spat. 'So you can stay down *here*.'

Honestly, she's so unreasonable. And mean! If I didn't just have a cheap lousy Walkman with flat batteries I wouldn't have been forced to lie.

Frankie's house is no better. It's crawling with younger Maloneys. And being Catholic, Mrs M is even stricter than Mum. She's got this little plastic font on the wall by her front door, and she drenches the kids in Holy Water whenever they go out. I bet she washes Frankie's underpants in it too. That would explain a lot!

At least she still thinks I'm a nice girl. She's always asking me when I'm going to be 'received into the Faith'. She hasn't cottoned on yet that I've outgrown my Catholic phase, and I haven't the heart to tell her.

I just can't believe that stuff about the Pope never getting anything wrong. You've only to see him on the telly kissing some foreign airport's tarmac to know that's not true. What about the germs?

You'd think things would be easier now that Frankie's got his motorbike. We could get out into the country and run romantically through cornfields or something. But he won't even let me on it. He says it's cos he hasn't got a spare helmet and he doesn't want my 'skull caved in'. He's *so* unromantic.

If only the Maloneys weren't so good looking. Every time I'm about to tell him I'm really fed up, I look at his big baby blues and lose my nerve. He's more drop-dead gorgeous than any mere male has the right to be. You should see those lovely black curls of his these days. His hair's short at the back but with this tiny little pigtail at the nape of his neck . . .

Ouch! Everyone goes on about fellas and sexual frustration but what about *us*??

Still, I will bear in mind your useful suggestion about taking Frankie baby-sitting. Amanda's always said, 'No boys – they can't be trusted.' But seeing as she trusts me so much, maybe I can sneak Frankie in.

As for your troubles – cheer up, Jean. There's hope for your nose yet. You're only 16 so maybe it's still growing.

I'm impressed you're now thinking of becoming a plastic surgeon. But I really wouldn't know if that means you can perform a do-it-yourself nose extension. You're the scientific one. I'm just glad you've rediscovered some ambition.

Gotta run – revision calls.

Yuck.

With love,

Maxine

PS What do you mean you *still* need to know more about my 'leaving home plans' before making a decision? I thought you'd agreed it was a great idea. Now you want a complete blueprint. Let's take one thing at a time – ie exams.

Anyway, there's not much to plan. It'll be a cinch.

April 26th

Dear Jean,

I'm horrified that you think I'm treating Frankie like a sex object. As I politely pointed out to your brother when *he* tried it on, 'Me, I go for a bloke's mind. Yours is in your trousers, so push off.'

That animal to whom you're so tragically related may have a car and loads of money now he's working for your parents, but Bob the Dog's idea of a charming conversation seems to be, 'How about it?'

I'm sorry I haven't told you about this before. I know you hate your brother too, but I didn't want to ruin your relationship completely.

Frankie, in contrast, is a gentleman. He's kind, he's funny, and when he's not talking about carburettors, he's interesting. He even wants to spend a year in Africa as a volunteer once he's finished his training. I'm not sure that what Rwanda needs most is painters and decorators, but it *is* a nice thought.

So you're wrong. It's not just because of Frankie's pigtail, or his smile, or the way he looks in his leather jacket that I like him.

Those just *help*.

I do hope you and I aren't going to get into one of those stupid competitive things about boyfriends, just because I've got one and you haven't. It's not your loss, it's *theirs*. Anyway, as mature intellectuals we should know better than to let such petty differences come between us.

So what *is* this drivel you wrote about suddenly feeling

24

'desperate . . . my nose can't wait any longer'? I'm stun-
ned. I can't believe you're wavering again and thinking
of giving up school, just so you can work and save up
for a nose job. Your nose is *fine*, Jean. It's where you take
it that's the problem.

You never go *anywhere* where you can meet boys! Well
– not suitable ones. Your Red Cross group is all girls,
the Whippet's Welcome all lushes, and at your Ashton-
under-Lyne Industrial History seminars you're *bound* only
to meet anoraks or crumblies.

You rightly loathe your brother's mates but I'm mysti-
fied why you won't date anyone at school. So OK, you
don't want to be like the other girls, dissolving their
brain cells while they snivel and sigh over some pimply
class mate. But I can't believe a classroom romance would
interfere *that* much with physics revision.

So chin up Jean (your nose will look bigger that
way) and think of your advantages. You're at least two
stone lighter than me *and* you've got cheekbones. Also
think of all the fellas you'll meet when you move to
London this summer. This is just a small famine before
the feast.

I just wish I could survive without quite so *much*
feasting – on Smarties that is. I was passing the newsagent
yesterday and Mr Habib sold me half a dozen boxes at
half price cos they were past their sell-by date. Now I'm
at least two ounces heavier – as well as broke. He's
heartless. He's made me lose my self-control.

Your getting-fatter-again friend,

Max

Dear Jean,

I knew it! You *are* a genius! I agree ten pounds is a tiny price for Bob the Dog to pay for our silence. I'm just not sure about you keeping half. I am the one he leched over, after all. And the one who's broke with nowhere to go.

Still, I'm glad to hear you're now 99.9 per cent sure you're coming with me — if only to get away from that slime-ball.

What a confused girl you are, Jean. One minute your only aim in life is to be a barmaid with a boyfriend. The next, you want really worthwhile things — like studying medicine and living with me.

Actually, I'm just as up and down myself. Why haven't we outgrown our hormones yet? I don't want to go out to work but, if I'm honest, I hate school too. It's revolting right now. All revision, exam nerves and AIDS. I'm sick of AIDS and I haven't even got it.

The teachers think they're so subtle with their 'cross-curricular' approach. You know, working in nooky-inspired germs every chance they get:

GEOGRAPHY
Bits of the world where AIDS is worst. Bits of the world that grow rubber, so your bits won't fall off.
MATHS
If the HIV virus has a mean incubation period of eight years, and 10.3 girls sleep with 0.9 infected males, what are their chances of gaining a Maths PhD?

ENGLISH
Ode to a Condom. Explain in your own words the impact of AIDS on love poetry.
BIOLOGY
How to reproduce while encased in rubber.

What an age to be young in, eh? I know it's important really, but sometimes I think the wrinklies are *glad* about AIDS. Anything to stop us having some fun. They don't really care about the infected babies in Romania or gay men.

Dad's one of the worst culprits. Since he began his mental decline and started reading the *Sun* – a sure sign of brain damage if you ask me – he's even started parroting their prejudices about 'the gay plague' and 'ginger beers'.

Much use his macho talk is to Mum. The other night, after she'd been at her Spanish gut-rot, the sherry started talking.

'He doesn't even know I'm a woman any more, Maxine,' she cried.

I suppose that means she isn't getting any.

What a disgusting thing to tell your daughter. What makes her think I'm interested in sex anyway?

I suppose AIDS is enough to put anyone off though. Especially Frankie. His lot (Roman Catholics, I mean) don't even allow condoms for contraception, never mind AIDS. That's another reason I've never converted.

Got to go now – it's the end of my free period for revision.

Thanks again for the fiver. I know you feel we shouldn't be greedy – but perhaps you should advise Bob that this was just the first instalment?

Much love,

Max

The Night before the Day of Reckoning
April 30th

Dear Jean,

I'm sorry you think 'my' plans to fleece your family – as you so delicately put it – are immoral. It was your brainwave in the first place.

I'm even more shocked to hear you expressing such fraternity with Bob the Dog. It must be an aberration brought on by exam anxiety.

I'm suffering from Examitis too, Jean, so you could be kinder. After all, it's your fault I'm so behind with my revision – I've spent most of my free periods at school writing to you.

This morning I realised there's just one month till our exams start! I've vowed to spend three hours a night revising from now on, but it's ten o'clock already and I haven't done a thing. I'm in too much of a state about my first-ever job interview tomorrow at Marks and Sparks. I don't know what to worry about more – failing the interview or passing it. I mean all I want is a summer and Saturday job, not the permanent knicker-selling career Dad's got his heart set on for me. But what if my natural genius shines through, despite my best efforts to suppress it, and they offer to make me a manager on the spot.

Dad would never forgive me if I turned that down.

Sue always says you should Dress for Success, so I've decided to limit my chances by wearing my school uniform and Doc Martens.

If I can still fit into my uniform, that is. Tonight Mum made me sit down and eat a huge tea – all fatty chips and cottage pie – because 'you can't study on an empty stomach and you've got a big day tomorrow'. The whole thing was *swimming* in grease. I had to do a hundred sit-ups just to work some of it off.

Then I came down to find Mum at the kitchen table, drafting yet another big chunk of unwanted advice to that smarmy MP, Virginia Bottomley. Since the demise of her heroine, Mrs Thatch, Mum's adopted 'Virginia' as her new Tory soul sister.

This letter was all about how she agrees with 'absolutely everything' the party stands for – except some minor details like destroying public transport, cutting Dad's benefits, threatening her hospital with closure and forcing her 'dear bright youngest daughter' (that's me) out to work just so they can 'make ends meet'.

I know because she insisted I sit down and correct her spelling. I suppose studying for eight GCSEs *is* less important than my mum telling Mrs Bumley how to transform their treasured party.

'I know you will open your heart,' she confidently ended, 'and help change these policies because, like Lady Thatcher and myself, you are a fellow woman and a mother.'

I told Mum that Mrs T used to beat up Cabinet Ministers just for disagreeing with her about the weather. But her faith is as indestructible as her pies.

'They were only against her,' Mum insisted, 'Because they're men – and chauvinists.' She really thinks these Tory women will listen to her because they all wear tights.

I ask you!

She obviously hasn't learnt any lessons from history. And neither have I. I'd better get a move on and start

29

studying. Here's to becoming a bundle of nerves! At least it's meant to speed up your metabolism.

Love,

Max

Hornsey

May 1st
The REAL May Day
Up the Workers

Dearest Jean,

I know it's not my turn to write but I am SO miserable. Today I got a job, got fat, and finally faced the fact that I live in a broken home.

I woke up this morning with my eyes on stalks and my stomach in knots. But did my family care? Forget it. Mum and Dad specially picked this morning for a fight so loud that Amanda next door came round to say they were interrupting her Greet-The-Day Meditation.

It was so awful that on my way to Marks this morning I gave up on breaking my addiction and snuck into Mr Habib's. He took one look at my taut, tense face and didn't even ask what I wanted. He just said, 'How many?'

'Got my job interview today,' I croaked.

He had to hand over four packets of M&M's (I've changed my fix) before I relaxed. I only had enough for one packet so he let me have one free for luck and the rest on tick.

Sometimes I think Mr Habib is my only friend.

Things were so different a year ago. Last May Day, we were all so happy. Dad was still a shop steward and busy organising that great Demo to save London buses and his job. He even wore that badge I made him – you know, the one that says, 'I'm a Mindless Militant and proud of it'. Then after breakfast, he made Sue and me march round the kitchen table singing The Red Flag! In our house, we always used to celebrate May the First that way. Daft really, but I liked it.

Today, Mum couldn't get Dad out of bed even when she was making it. That's what the row was about.

'What have I got to get up for?' he yelled. 'You vote Tory! You must be happy with the State of the Nation. Me, I'm staying in my pit.'

Once the furore had subsided, I reminded Mum that to-day was the day I give up on my life and give in to Marks, and she managed a quick hug and a 'Good Luck'. But Dad didn't surface before I left and Sue was too busy giving me grief about nicking her tights to offer any support.

It was downhill all the way after that – literally. Going into the interview room, I was so nervous that I tripped over my feet and practically fell on to the personnel lady's desk. After that, I didn't have to work too hard at seeming less impressive than I am – whenever she asked me a question I'd go all beetroot-faced and stuttery. But I still think she should have offered me a manager's job – I'd got it all worked out how to turn her down without hurting her feelings.

Obviously she hasn't got any – she said I could have a measly summer sales job and 'maybe' a permanent one *if* Marks is satisfied with me. What if *I'm* not satisfied with them? She didn't even think about that.

Oh well, at least it'll be my and Frankie's anniversary

soon and I've got that surprise present to look forward to. He's been saving for *ages* now!

I'm too hard on him – he *is* romantic really. I wonder if his gift will be gold – like his heart?

Yours in hope,

Maxine

Hornsey

'Spring Bank Holiday'
The government's prissy
version of May Day
and my and Frankie's anniversary

Dear Jean,

Today I went on Frankie's bike for the first time! I looked like a complete prat. And Frankie's present to me was about as romantic as period pains.

Like you suggested, I went for the casual but ravishable look for our Big Day. I nicked Sue's new mini skirt, and wore my biggest earrings plus this dead tight T shirt.

Then Frankie arrived and the first thing he said was, 'Go and take those clothes off.' I nearly swooned.

Unfortunately, the second thing he said was, 'Put your jeans on instead – and this.'

'This' was a bundle of newspaper shoved into my arms. My present.

He said he was sorry about the wrapping, but the parcel was too big for gift paper.

'What did you get?' I hear you gasp. I'll tell you. A ninth-hand crash helmet emblazoned 'Mods Are Cool'

32

and an ancient bike jacket of indescribable ugliness. You'll realise how seriously sad it is when I tell you that my dad *loves* it. 'Blimey,' he drooled, 'I had one just like that in my scooter days.'

I think it's the same one – it certainly fits his 6′ better than my 5′ 7″. I could fit a spare tyre up the front and the cuffs practically reach my knees. It's shapeless, it's not even leather but 1970s 'leather look' plastic, and – most embarrassing of all – it's *maroon*.

Dad must have caught the expression on my face, because when Frankie was out of the room he said, 'You just be grateful, Madam. You've no idea how much this gear costs, even second hand. Frankie obviously cares about your body even if you don't.'

I was about to say, 'Har! Little do you know!', when Dad started showing me his motorbike scars. They were so revolting I gave in.

You'd have thought he was giving Frankie my hand in marriage, the way he announced, 'Now you've got her all kitted out safely, lad, once I've checked your bike, you can take my little girl out for a spin.'

Then he spent ages inspecting Deirdre and having some completely incomprehensible conversation with Frankie about spark plugs and throttles. Meanwhile I stood by in this mangy old maroon thing feeling like a right lemon and looking like a giant plum.

Mum hit the nail on the head when she said, 'Men! I haven't seen your dad that interested in anything since Number Twelve's underwear catalogue was posted to us by mistake.'

To be fair, going on the bike was *brilliant*, once I forgot about the motorists laughing at me. So was snuggling up to Frankie's back, and clinging to his hips! I caught on dead quick how to bend my body when we were turning corners, and I loved feeling so free and fast and brave — even if it was Frankie doing the driving.

I'd like to report that we went somewhere romantic. Frankie *meant* to take us out into the country, but unfortunately he can never skip a skip. Seeing as it was a Bank Holiday, the Do-It-Yourself brigade were out in force. We barely made it out of N8.

Since Frankie took up painting and decorating, he's become a right scavenger. He collects ugly old-fashioned things like the fireplaces people tear out once they can afford nice modern pretend ones. Then he flogs them to The Toffs, like Amanda and Nathan next door. Mum says it's an act of vandalism what they've done to their house. They've ripped off all the plastic cladding.

By the time we'd poked through most of North London's rubbish, we were both covered in plaster dust and gasping. So we ended up at, you've guessed it, The Three Boring Brewers.

I thought the drink might make Frankie sentimental, but being ever so sensible he even toasted me in non-alcohol beer. If you can call it a toast. He squeezed my knee under the table and said, 'Here's to us — you're a really good mate, Max.'

Do you think I'm on a loser, Jean?

I did get some real tongue-hugging at the door. And on the bike today, even though we're not supposed to get off on these things, being Feminists, I really got a thrill from Frankie being so calm, confident and . . . ohhh, *masculine.*

But just how long, Jean, can a girl survive on rubbish skips and saliva?

Yours,
confused,

Maxine

PS   Why have you wimped out? I haven't heard a word from you in weeks about our flat-share.

Hornsey

May 9th

Dear Jean,

I appreciate your worrying about me and Frankie, but NOT about you and me leaving home. We are NOT 'too young to take care of ourselves'. Try telling that to children doing a full day's manual work in Africa or China. So says Dad, whenever I dare say I'm shattered after seven hours of Haringey Girls.

Seriously, Jean, I do sometimes wonder if you aren't under-deprived. I know your family moved back up North to rediscover their 'roots', but what's so barncake and Vimto about your dad's designer clogs?

He's always on about 'soft, spineless Southerners', but recently I've shown far more spine than you. Nothing personal, but your objection that 'flats are hard to come by' makes you sound so wet I feel like sending you a towel.

You obviously aren't in the habit of studying news-agents' windows. Mr Habib's is full of cards from people wanting council house exchanges — hence my brilliant idea.

Mum and Dad won't need a two-bedroomed house once I go and Sue gets married. So I'm going to suggest they swap ours for some old couple's one-bedroomed flat. Then M & D could move out, and we'll stay here to be the oldies' live-in housekeepers.

It'd be great all round. We'd be saving some poor frail oldies from an institution, Mum and Dad would get that change of scenery they're always on about, and I'd prove I can be independent, rent-free.

Also, Frankie would still only be five doors down.

So, please stop fretting over minor details, Jean. You need to have a larger vision, like me.

I do hope the real reason you're getting cold feet isn't that new boy in your Red Cross class. Fancying a fella just because he 'did a good tourniquet' on you sounds distinctly kinky to me.

Besides, you'll meet loads of fascinating types once we boldly strike out on our own.

In fact, I'm bound to meet some tomorrow. It's that drama group audition I was telling you about. So keep your fingers crossed for me, Jean.

And your toes! Here's hoping I 'break a leg' as we say in the acting profession. Thanking you in advance.

Your about-to-be-discovered best friend,

Maxie

May 10th

*(That's how you say Artistic Hornsey with a French
accent)

Dear Jean,

I know it's not my turn to write but I've *got* to share
the good news or I'll burst. MY THEATRICAL
CAREER IS ABOUT TO BEGIN! Yes, I passed the
audition.

Actually, everybody did. Amanda says she wants to
'open up the Arts to all', so all seven of us who auditioned
got picked.

There were lots more hopefuls around at the beginning, about 30 I'd guess, including Rosie, Grace and
Anna from school. I'd made them come along as protec-
tion. Just in case anyone laughed at me in my homeless
daffodil gear.

I don't *think* anyone did – it was a really fun night. To
start, Amanda made us chant and wriggle around on the
floor. Unfortunately, Rosie and co immediately copped
out, and Grace had to be carried out snorting between
them. Perhaps she really was having a fit, but I suspect
they just couldn't handle that much Art.

It is sad – I used to feel those girls were like me,
cultural and sensitive. Well, at Haringey Girls they're
outsiders too. Obviously Alienation does not inspire
everyone to become an Artiste.

Most of the other kids left saying they had to go to
the loo and never came back. One girl walked out in

tears. She said she hadn't spent hours getting ready just to ladder her lurex tights crawling over the floor.

I know how she felt. As you know I've spent weeks practising 'I wandered lonely as a cloud' and looking like a daffodil. Fortunately, I cottoned on as soon as I got there that this wasn't going to be any boring traditional audition. So I tried to act as though I always wear a yellow body suit, green leggings and lug around a cardboard box.

Still, even an adaptable Bohemian type like me was a bit thrown when Amanda asked us to act out being born. As I said, I was only nought at the time so I really can't remember much.

I must have put on a good show though because lots of the kids who'd chickened out were watching through the window, and they laughed their heads off.

My first fans!

The other kids who passed the audition seem nice enough, even if they do have daft names like Caspar and Jolyon. I felt a bit shy because they seemed to know all about Performance Art. (That's what Amanda says we'll be doing – not just words, but movement and mime and sounds.) But Cas (Caspar) put me at my ease – he even asked for my phone number! He said he really liked the look of my crowd and maybe we could all get together some time?

Our show is for the Hornsey Festival in August (FAME! Book now while seats last!). It won't have a script, because that's 'undemocratic' and Amanda wants it to be 'spontaneous and improvised', ie made up. She says it can be about anything we like, as long as it's set in the womb and 'an indictment of the alienation of Modern Day Youth' – whoever he is, when he's at home.

'Poofy middle-class rubbish,' said Dad, when I came home all excited. Straightaway prejudiced, just because

'That Mad Meditating Cuthbert woman' is involved. He still hasn't forgiven the Cuthberts for being the first Toffs to move in when our area stopped being Deprived and started having what estate agents call 'Potential'.

He reckons it's the 'hanging plants brigade' who are destroying 'local working-class culture'. Though what's so cultured about furry dice I don't know – especially when you hang them in the kitchen window cos you haven't got a car.

With Dad in this mood, it doesn't seem diplomatic to unveil my great plan about moving. Besides, I've got to get on with my geography revision. (It's not that I don't have better things to do on a Friday night, but panic has given me new dedication.) As long as I'm not asked anything about China, India, North America or Australasia I should be all right.

I just wanted you to be the first to know . . .

A star is about to be born!

Hereafter follows my autograph:

Does that look anything like Maxine Harrison? It isn't supposed to. Rich people always have unreadable signatures so no one can forge their cheques.

May 15th

Dear Jean,

Your reply received at last. All right, all right. If it makes you happy, you can try flat-sharing just for the summer to 'see how it goes'. Don't sound so shirty. I've got nothing against you being 'sensible' – as you put it.

Personally, I'd top myself if a friend's mother described me as 'a good influence'. But that, Jean, I regret to say, is how my mother now sees you. You're Ms Goody Two Shoes.

Don't you miss being written off as a bad influence? That's got far more street cred.

Of course, you never really were anything of the kind. I just used to blame everything on you. Somehow Mum's finally cottoned on.

But I know you do have a wayward streak deep down. So – when are you arriving? I plan to have everything sorted out by my birthday, so I'll expect you that weekend. You can throw a belated 16th birthday party for me, and we'll make it our house-warming do, too.

Sadly, I've suffered a slight setback in getting us a house to warm. Tonight I told Mum and Dad about my brilliant plan for them to move out. I showed them all the ads I'd jotted down from people wanting to move off some estate in N9. It sounds like a really swish place. They've got all the mod cons – even burglar alarms and reinforced doors.

Dad was only half listening as usual, and Mum just giggled.

'Maxine,' she said, 'are you SURE you've done enough geography revision? Don't you know where N9 is?'

Seeing as Mum was so tickled, I decided to press my advantage.

'We're N8,' I replied, 'So N9 can't be that far away. Even if it is, you like walking for your figure, and it's not as though Dad needs to be near his work – he hasn't got any.'

I don't know why, but that set Dad off. Suddenly he was ranting and raving that even if he wanted to move to Broadwater Farm and get burgled or burnt out, he couldn't.

'Because Your Mother has put me in hock with a rotten mortgage for the next 25 years.'

I admit, I'd forgotten that detail. But that was still no excuse for him to call me selfish, immature and silly. They're the selfish ones. They're the ones who got married without a decent living parent between them, just so Sue and I wouldn't have grandparents. I'd grown really keen on the idea of having two oldies around to spoil. Now I'll go to my grave never having made Ovaltine for someone I could call Gran.

So – it looks like we'll have to rent after all. *C'est la vie.*

How's your French getting on by the way? I know I was practically fluent last year, when I was weak-kneed about that snobby French boy, but with all these worries on my plate, I'm even forgetting how to swear *en français.*

Quelle horreur!

Love,

Max

May 18th

Dear Jean,

Please stop freaking out! I said I'd move out on my birthday and June 28th's only six weeks away but, trust me, everything's under control.

I'll start looking for a flat as soon as the exams are over. For now, I'm concentrating on my finances. Yes, it's official. Marks definitely do want me to start this summer, and if you play your cards right there could be a job for you too. I'll happily give you a reference, in return for a small commission.

I don't mean to be grasping but when you're practically alone in the world you have to be. Things are looking up, though. I've worked out that if I can persuade Amanda and Nathan to go out more than once a week, I can count on at least two nights baby-sitting just for them.

I'll just remind them how horrible their Little Sods are and how their marriage will improve if they leave them more often with a nice, child-loving girl like me.

In all, I should coin in about one hundred pounds a week!

My budget is as follows:

RENT   £25
(Well, the average rent's more like £50 per week but you'll be sharing my gaff and paying half.)

FARES   nil
(It'll be good for our figures if we walk everywhere.)

FOOD   £25
(Crispbread and TV dinners don't cost that much.)

ENTERTAINMENT   £20
(We'll deserve a bit of fun after working hard all week.)

MISCELLANEOUS   £15
(Hair gel, presents, cassettes and other essentials.)

CLOTHES   £20
(At last! No more of Sue's hand-me-downs!)

MAKE-UP   £5
SAVINGS   £10
                     ──────
                     £100 exactly!

And Mum says I've no idea what anything costs.

The savings, by the way, are for when the summer's over and we're studying again. You see, I've thought of everything.

I hope you're impressed by me. I am.

With much love,

Your soon-to-be flatmate
Max the Mighty Money Machine

Dear Jean,

Drama group tonight was a complete cringe. The acting bit was OK, at least crawling around the floor must have burned off some of the seven fish fingers Mum forced me to eat for tea. But then Amanda made everyone sit round in a circle to plan how we could make the Dead Crucial Company's show 'a true community production'.

What that meant was, how could our mums and dads help out?

That didn't faze the others. Jolyon, who'll be playing the Midwife, said his dad was a graphic designer so he could make the posters. The mother of Charlotte (the Amniotic Fluid) is a journalist, so she'll mastermind publicity. Jonathan the Contractions said his accountant dad could help him keep the group's books, and Victoria the Womb offered her mum as our technical advisor (she's a gynaecologist). By the time that Liberty (the Life Force) and her brother Cas, the gorgeous-looking Umbilical Cord, had signed up their parents' Whole Foods Café for interval catering, I was in a real panic. What could my unemployed bus conductor father and bed pan emptying mother possibly offer The Arts?

Then I remembered that Mum is quite good at sewing. Well, she's had tons of experience taking down hems. So I said she could be in charge of costume.

There was an awful silence. Then Caspar laughed, and Jolyon tittered. Soon everyone was roaring, Amanda too.

Finally Victoria took pity on me. Maxine, she said,

44

you haven't been listening. What on earth do you imagine unborn babies wear?

I was about to joke, 'Pampers Nappies', when suddenly it hit me.

WE WON'T BE WEARING ANY CLOTHES AT ALL!

Well, except for body stockings, and Amanda's going to borrow those from her college. It seems her students are always doing shows without clothes on, because 'costumes subtract from the message'.

What about the excess baggage on my thighs? How am I going to subtract from those? Yes – my GCSE props are showing.

Unless I lose a load of weight fast, I can't possibly let Frankie come. He'll never want to get to know me better if he sees me in something figure hugging. Nor will Cas. Don't tell Frankie, but just thinking of Cas encased in nylon gives me goose pimples all over. His name is the only wimpy thing about him – the rest of him is tall and tanned with long blond tangled curls, just like a surfer's.

I'm not REALLY being disloyal. I mean, fancying your co-star is a well-known occupational hazard. You're so thrown together. Interconnected, really – especially when, like me, you're the foetus and he's your umbilical cord.

Actually, I haven't a clue what the show's about. Being dragged screaming out of the womb by a whopping great pair of forceps hardly constitutes a graceful acting début. But Amanda says it will grow on me. 'Yeah, like mould,' snorted Dad, when I foolishly confided in him.

He's such a philistine. He won't even cough up my £3 a week sub for the group, which he could easily afford if he gave up smoking his horrible old rollies. I said he'd be helping his health, not just The Arts, but he just said I should concentrate on my exams, not arty farty time wasting.

Mum stuck up for me. She said learning lines wasn't arty farty, it was a really good way of improving my memory. I didn't have the heart to tell her that all I get to say is 'Push'.

Mum's niceness quickly evaporated when I told her she'd volunteered to sell fifty tickets at her hospital. 'Don't you think I've enough on my plate,' she said, 'having to feed fifty people at your sister's wedding?'

I'd come in to find her, Sue and Mum's mate Linda drawing up yet another of their Wedding Lists. You wouldn't believe the hours they spend fretting over these things. Lists of food, lists of guests, lists of the presents my greedy sister wants, lists of hymns, booze, things to buy and things to decorate.

Personally, I think it's all just an excuse for Mum to order more rubbish from Linda's catalogue and get addled with her. After Sue had carefully poured a few sherries down them, Mum even agreed that we had to redecorate the front room for the Big Day.

That set Dad off. He says if Sue was a decent daughter she'd be living in sin to spare him the expense.

Dorky Derek's parents are chipping in, because they know otherwise all anyone will get to eat is half a twiglet. But Dad still moans on. I think the sickest thing is him spending all that dosh selling off Sue when he won't even invest in something the world really needs, ie launching my acting career.

Just wait till I'm famous and interviewed by the *Sun*. I'll tell them all about my tragic childhood.

I'm so glad *I'm* not bitter and twisted.

With love, to the only person who really understands me,

Maxine

46

Dearest Jean,

I can't resist sending you this. I scribbled it today during English after I realised I hadn't a single thing left to learn about *The Merchant of Venice*. It may not get me an A in my exams, but it's good practice for when I'm rich and famous and fighting off journalists. It's the COR! WORRA MEANIE! interview that I'm going to give exclusively to the *Sun*. That way Dad's sure to see it.

TORRID TEMPTRESS Maxine Harrison yesterday confessed that her fearsome father nearly ruined her career.

Fighting back tears, the sexy superstar, 21, recalled her yearning youth.

'I bet my dad's proud now I'm on the telly,' she sobbed, 'but where was the old hypocrite with my £3 when I needed it?'

Just £3, she explained, was needed for her to join the world-famous Dead Crucial Company, then poor and struggling in 'horrid Hornsey'.

'But my dad's so mean,' she cried, 'He wouldn't even give you a Kleenex after he'd used it.'

Britain's favourite actress described her LIFE OF HORROR with the Hornsey Hoarder.

• He'd TURN OFF THE TELLY when she was watching it. 'He'd say it was because it was past my bedtime, but I know it was just to save electricity.'

• He'd snort 'I SHOULD COCOA' when she asked him for money for HAIR GEL.

• He FORCED HER to leave school to sell SLEAZY UNDIES when she was only 16.

For years now, the brunette bombshell's father hasn't been seen. Today, your caring sharing super sizzling *Sun* finally tracked down Mr Dave Harrison, 47, to his home in a cardboard box beneath the arches at Charing Cross.

'After I forced my daughter to leave home,' explained this broken man, 'I went downhill. She was the light of my life, and I hadn't realised it.

'Now I'm on skid row, and I deserve it. My only pleasure is watching Maxine every night on the telly through the windows of electrical appliance shops.'

Maxine's sister, housewife Mrs Sue Dowdy, was unable yesterday to comment.

'I'd love to talk to you about my wonderful sister's glamorous career,' she said through the letter box, 'But my husband wants his potatoes mashed.'

But Maxine's mother today confirmed, 'Her dad was a right skinflint. He never believed in her. But I did. I sold 50 tickets at work just for her first show.'

An overjoyed Maxine today thanked the *Sun* for reuniting her with her long-lost father.

'My dad's right,' she said, 'I shouldn't forgive him.

'But because he's said sorry for the first time in his life, I'll think about it.'

Should merciful Maxine forgive her father? Or should she kick him when he's down? Ring our *Sun* COR! WORRA MEANIE! line to register your vote NOW.

Isn't that great? It just goes to show that, whatever Dad says, studying Shakespeare does have its uses. I wrote this after memorising Portia's 'The quality of mercy is not strained' speech, which is all about forgiveness.

48

Har! That'll show the old miser!
With much love,

Maxie (the Brunette Bombshell)

The Bunker

May 28th

Dear Jean,

Today it hit me. Like a sledgehammer. Only one week to go!

We went over our exam timetable this morning – it's terrifying! Just my luck to have to start with biology – my worse subject of all. But I shouldn't do *too* badly – I've revised practically everything. Except, gulp, maths, physics, history . . . and biology.

Bat-Face looked grimmer than ever as she read out all the rules. I've started having nightmares about oversleeping and missing an exam. Or getting my times muddled up. Let's face it, *anything* could happen. What with not having anywhere to live once it's all over, I'll probably end up with eczema like Dad. Then even Frankie won't want to know. I'm *so* stressed out!

I am trying to stay calm in spite of everything. But all I can eat is cottage cheese and M&M's. At least it's a balanced diet.

In anxious solidarity,

Max

49

May 30th

Dear Jean,

I should be revising for biology. Instead, I'm round at
Amanda's baby-sitting, and even though it's only 9.30
I'm shattered. The Little Sods have finally shut up – I
said if they didn't, the Tooth Fairy would pull out all
their teeth. But lullabying them to sleep was the easy
part. It was fetching Amanda's groceries that really did
me in.

It sounded a nice easy number, doing Amanda's supermarket run in return for her waiving my drama group
fee. It's what she calls 'skill sharing' – she teaches me to
move like a foetus, and I take care of her Little Sods. I
thought I'd enjoy pretending to be a Gym Slip Mum.
But by the time Seb and Allie had revolved me out the
revolving doors, they had me believing in the merits of
post-natal abortion.

For a start, I hadn't counted on Seb wanting to ride
in the trolley's toddler seat. He *is* eight. But Alexandra
said I had to let him, because their parents believe in
children's Freedom and Choice. Two aisles later, Seb *chose*
to get free, but his pig fat legs were stuck between the
bars. It took me, two assistants and half a pound of butter
to pull him out.

By that stage, I was all for grabbing the first tins I saw
and making a quick getaway. But Allie made me inspect
every single thing for additives, animal rights and excess
packaging. She's only nine, but she's already a 'Health
Conscious Politically Aware Shopper'.

I was lectured the whole way round. The Cuthberts

50

will only touch 'dolphin friendly' tuna, fruit and veg in season, coffee grown by workers' co-ops and 'ozone friendly' oven cleaners.

I'm all for being green, Jean, but when I found myself checking for monosodium glutamate in the J Cloths I realised I was off shopping for life.

How am I going to cope when I leave home? I must find out about shopping delivery services. I've seen them advertised.

All this grief MUST be worth more than my £3 drama group fee. Amanda's all for Ending Exploitation as long as it's far away and she can carry on exploiting ME, the girl next door. I only agreed to baby-sit, too, if I could bring along 'one of the Maloneys'. I *meant* Frankie, but he's out. So I ended up with Imelda.

Imelda's great, but these days there's a distance between us. I keep wanting to ask her advice about Frankie and me but I don't dare. She's his sister, *and* a religious fanatic. She's joined the Roman Catholic Feminists now. She says it's her last chance of becoming the first woman Pope. I don't suppose Popes-to-be are particularly interested in how to get a bloke frisky.

It's a shame – we were much closer when I was thinking of becoming a Catholic. Or is it me going out with her brother that's come between us? I dunno. But just one hour with me and the Little Sods proved enough for her. After Seb rifled through her bag and wolfed down all her unorganic Maltesers she suddenly remembered she had a karate class to go to.

So here I am on my own, re-reading your letter, and feeling jealous about your progress with Red Cross Jake. He sounds really nice – I wish he'd put my arm in a sling. That bit about him smoothing down your plaster of Paris sounds dead romantic.

Write soon. In fact, seeing as we're practically flatmates

as well as best friends, please send me *explicit* details by the next post.

Love

Max

Hornsey

June 4th

Dearest Jean,

I am replying straightaway to your heartbreaking plea for help. DON'T PANIC! I'm quite sure you can't get pregnant from doing THAT. My grasp of biology is really quite good, even if the only diagram I managed to draw in my exam today was of a hydra doing a somersault. ☝︎☖☖

If I'd been asked about useful things like the human reproductive system or the effect of alkali on zits, I'd have been recognised for the Marie Curie I am.

As it is, I have undoubtedly failed.

I am so depressed. I'm probably going to fail EVERYTHING.

Dad's right, it's all my own fault. I should have spent more time revising and less time acting and revving it up with Deirdre.

Farewell my dreams of RADA, Drury Lane and gracing the silver screen. Wood Green Marks and Sparks probably won't even want me now.

Poor old Rosie's in a worst funk than me. After today's paper, she was all for grabbing her dad's bolt cutters and leading a raid to retrieve the evidence from Bat-Face's vault. Thank God I managed to convince her to have a therapeutic facial instead.

Sometimes sharing a bedroom with Sue has its advantages. It's amazing the amount of cosmetics that girl has. After a two-hour session – defoliator, mud-pack, blackhead hunt, etc – we'd erased every line of concern from Rosie's face.

Maybe I could become a beautician, if you don't need a biology GCSE. I've just about given up on ambition. I'm just glad I'm not alone in my suffering and that we're all in this together.

Luv,

Max

PS   I hope you come on soon.

Hornsey

June 7th

Dear Jean,

Thank you for your reassuring phone call. I'm sorry you think I insulted your morals. How was I to know it's exam stress that's stopped your periods? I'm so stressed myself I no longer even THINK about sex, not even whether Bat-Face has ever done it or not.

You did also mention that worry straight after going into ecstasies about Jake the Rake. How was I to know that the activities leading to the release of the hand-brake

53

in his mother's car were entirely unrelated? Not everyone spends their first date sling-making.

OF COURSE I know you're too sensible to get carried away. Other than to the bottom of a hill, that is.

Thank God you weren't parked on a very steep one.

I wish having my nose flattened on a dashboard was the worst of my worries. It's not even as if you've got much of one to flatten. I've suddenly realised it's only weeks till my birthday and I'm supposed to leave home. I've started checking flat rents in the local paper and they're AWFUL. About three times higher than I imagined.

So maybe I should honour Mum and Dad with my presence a bit longer. Of course I can't cope with them except in small doses, hence my brainwave. This could solve all my parents' problems – as well as mine.

With Sue moving out to become Mrs Derek, our room becomes just mine. I desperately need privacy and Mum and Dad endlessly bleat on about wanting Peace and Quiet. So I'll give them that, by converting my room into A BEDSIT!

If Mum buys me a mini-fridge, cooker, kettle and TV, I can be completely self-contained. Apart from having to share bathroom facilities and the front door, that is. If they feel that means I'm still in the way, Dad could build a staircase up the outside of the house. Then I could have my own separate entrance.

I expect they'd have to take out a second mortgage to pay for it but it would vastly improve the value of our house. They'd have rental income, too. In the long run it would pay for itself!

Naturally I'd invite you to be my flatmate.

A nice bit of building work would give Dad something to do – it might even 'restore his manhood', as Mum puts it. Then she could stop drooling over her soap opera pin-ups. She'd have you to replace the daughter she's losing. You'd have your best friend *and* your independence. Best of all, I'd be able to leave home without leaving home at all.

I know my Dad's irrational, but even he might see this makes sense.

So – keep your fingers crossed. I won't tell Dad tonight, because he's still smarting, poor sausage, from another job rejection letter. But he's always saying that book reading can't teach you common sense. When he sees that I've got gallons of 'common' and more to spare he'll probably even let me stay on at school.

With much love,

Max

PS   Do we *really* need a cooker? Maybe we should just eat take-aways and save on the washing up?

Or should I still let Mum cook our meals, so she doesn't feel rejected?

Sunday, June 9th

Dearest Jean,

Well, my great idea about the bed-sit went down like a cup of cold sick even though I brought it up (the idea, I mean) dead subtly.

I waited till Dad had stuffed his face and was all comfy in his armchair after tea. Then I pointed out this tragic story in today's papers about teenage runaways and said, 'Wouldn't it be sad if *I* ended up living in a cardboard

55

box?' Dad just grunted that I'd be too dozy to find one and went back to sleep.

Luckily, I wasn't relying on his sense of compassion to save the day. So I went for his greed instead. I did a really good sales pitch about the financial advantages to Property Owners of home improvements. Then I produced my plan of the bed-sit. Yes, I'd even done an architect's drawing, to make it easier for him to understand. (The curtains and pot plants I'd coloured in looked especially pretty.) I was just explaining about the outside staircase when Dad interrupted.

'When will you understand we don't have any money!' he bellowed. Then he embarked on one of his Cost of Living tirades. Mum ran in from the washing up and demanded, 'What have you done to upset your father this time?' She *always* takes his side.

I *told* them Frankie would help with the building work for free but that just made Dad worse. 'Don't you tell me how "good" he is with his hands,' he snarled, 'I wasn't born yesterday, I know what use he'd put them to if you had your own little love-nest.'

I was shocked by his filthy mind, I really was. How could I tell him my heart's breaking because Frankie is frigid?

I burst into tears and ran upstairs. Mum came up later with a cup of tea, but that upset me even more. She didn't even remember that my new anti-zit detox diet bans it. I started it yesterday to deal with the forest of pus on my face caused by exams, stress and overdosing on M&M's.

'I'm supposed to be on mineral water all this week,' I yelled, 'but you're too mean to buy me any!'

Maybe I did go a bit over the top, but that's no excuse for my own mother to tell me to leave home.

'Maybe that's the only way you'll find out how much

everything costs,' she said. And then she went back downstairs leaving me all alone to cry again. She's so cold-hearted. Just because I told her to naff off, and that she never wanted me anyway! Why didn't she *know* that meant I needed a cuddle?

Now I'll *have* to leave home. I've been ordered to.

I shouldn't be writing to you. I should be revising for history tomorrow. But I'm so upset I've picked one of my spots even though it wasn't ready.

Why do they set exams when you're tortured by raging hormones and a future on the street?

Thank God I've got you, the only person I know who doesn't call a magazine a book.

Love,

Max

PS I'm still puzzling about why Jake refused to take you to Casualty after you pranged your nose in his car. Are you *sure* it's a sign of 'social responsibility and tenderness' that he bandaged it himself, rather than 'waste NHS resources'?

I've had a dreadful thought. Maybe he's a Tory.

Dearest Jean,

No reply yet from you but I'll write anyway — just in case you're faintly worried about me or about to send a cardboard box by urgent post. Yes I do still have a home.

I am speaking to Mum again, just about. But only because she made an effort last night and gave me salad for tea. I came home in a state of shock from the history exam, let my knees buckle when she opened the door, and obviously needed pampering.

But like the Allies in 1918 (this is the only question I was good at), Mum won the war only to lose the peace. I was feeling all warm towards her, because for once she'd fed me only 290 calories (approx.), when she sat down, whipped out a crumpled chip bag covered with sums and destroyed me all over again.

My mother, the woman who's supposed to love me more than anyone in the whole world, had spent her day at the caff working out how much me staying on at school would cost her. *On the back of a bag reading Bert's Bangers Are Best*. Oh, the cynicism! No wonder I have no chance of becoming an Artiste.

I won't bore you with the painful details. School uniform, lunches, school trips, books, bus fares, etc. The mean git had even thrown in pens, pencils, pocket money (what happened to giving from *love*?), and (just to embarrass me), even £2 per month for . . . well, you know, *it*.

She had another list too, on a crumpled serviette, of Other Money Going Out (mortgage, etc.) versus Money Coming In. Dad's benefits, her caff and hospital earnings

. . . and Smarmy Sue's rent. Which left me, of course, as the Family Skiver.

She was trying to show me how the figures didn't add up, but my eyes were swimming so much I couldn't take them in. Anyway, she probably fixed them, like the government fiddles the unemployment ones. I know I'm 5' 7" but I couldn't *possibly* cost that much.

Then she tried to sugar the pill by saying maybe by next year Dad would have a job again, and I could go back to sixth form then. Meanwhile, if I worked full time at Marks, I'd be learning in The University of Life.

I couldn't believe this was my mum, who'd always told me to go for it; who'd wanted to be a top secretary but had ended up lumbered with a baby at seventeen instead.

It was sick. I felt so miserable that I even accepted an invitation to the pub from Smarmy Sue and Drippy Derek, just to get out of the house. I didn't realise: they too were in on the plot to destroy my artistic and intellectual potential.

Sue spent most of the time polishing her engagement ring, and shooting her best sarky look at three girls near by nursing halves.

'Look at them, the poor things,' she said. 'Grungey clothes, filthy trainers and not a man between them. That's what comes of staying on for A levels. Derek, darling – bring me another bacardi and coke.'

Of course Derek jumped to it. I've got to admit, Jean, for a moment I thought: maybe this is what it's all about. If I'd been with Frankie, we'd have been scrabbling through our pockets to see if we had enough for another lemonade and two straws.

Then Derek came back with a Perrier for me and doubles for himself and Sue. As he explained, grinning from ear to ear, 'We're celebrating, girl – my latest win.'

Do-or-Die Derek has got himself a new sideline, selling life insurance. He'd just earned a huge sum for scamming some poor newly widowed mother into an extra fifty quid a month. He'd told her the government was about to close down all children's homes. So what, he asked, would happen to her tragic orphans if she fell under a bus?

Sue looked on admiringly but I was appalled. 'Is that true about the kids' homes?' I asked.

Derek laughed so much he splattered half his vodka over his silk shirt.

'I dunno – I hope so! Silly cow.'

He meant the widow, not me, but I still hated him. And I suddenly felt proud of Frankie, sticking it out on his City and Guilds course, and of me. At least we've got Ideals.

What am I going to do, Jean? My family want me out sweeping chimneys as soon as possible. But if I give up my education I might end up like Sue. And seeing potential in someone like Derek??

I want upwards and OUT.

Help!

Write soon.

Instantly.

This minute.

Now.

Yours urgently,

Max

Dear J,

Merci beaucoup for your phone call last night. Those, I
devoutly hope, are the last words I will ever write in
French. No, I did *not* do well in the exam today.

I am so glad your examining board gave you exactly
the questions *you'd* revised for. It was so kind of you to
ring and tell me this, the night before my own Froggie
GCSE. I'm sure you meant well, too, in warning me not
to stay up all night to cram more vocab.

That is why, when expected to translate a passage about
a fancy restaurant meal into French, I failed abysmally. I
come from a deprived background, remember: I scarcely
know what *haute cuisine* is in English, never mind *français*.

'*Passez-moi* le OK sauce'. In culinary terms, Jean, that's
about my limit in either language.

Tant pis! I shouldn't blame you. I merely note, Jean,
how keen you are on ladling out unsolicited advice.

Let's change the subject. WHY are you still with that
Tory??? I was shocked rigid, Jean, by your confession
that Red Cross Jake IS of that perverted political per-
suasion.

I've been worrying about it all day. It probably explains
why I've failed French.

Only you could move to a depressed former mill town,
where even the police vote Labour, and end up with the
sole local Tory. It's no excuse, Jean, saying Jake is just
the Tory agent's *son*. If he's only in Red Cross because
it's a 'cost-cutting alternative to hospitals', he's *got it bad*.

I'm sure he *is* very good looking. But Hitler's girlfriend
probably thought that too!

No hard feelings. I just thought you should know I don't approve.

            With much love,

                Maxine

                        Haringey Girls' High

                                        Friday
                        9.40 am, free period for revision

Dear Jean,

I'm writing to apologise for my ratty letter. I felt guilty as soon as I'd posted it. If it hasn't arrived yet, TEAR IT UP, unopened, when it does.

I'd have rung you, but you know my dad. Even in an emergency like this he won't let me make long distance calls.

I just want you to know that I DO appreciate some of your advice. You know how you told me to get professional help for my personal problems? Well, yesterday after school I went to the Citizens Advice Bureau.

I told the lady there I'm destined to be a great star of stage and screen but my parents want me behind a bra counter. Unfortunately, she didn't seem to take my tragedy seriously. Perhaps I should have worn Sue's high heels instead of my Doc Martens, then I would have looked more ambitious.

She was a real do-gooder type, with an accent so posh she made the Queen sound Cockney. She said I could be helped to leave home if I was abused, and perked up when I told her I am, all the time. She grabbed some paper and started writing frantically. But when she realised I 'only' meant verbal abuse, plus the odd slap from Sadistic Sue, she chucked her notes in the bin.

I felt a real failure, too common to seem an Artiste, and too under-deprived to deserve help.

'Look,' I explained, 'I don't just want to be in soaps. I've got what it takes to play Macbeth.'

I thought she should see what the world would be missing, so I started on a dead good version of 'Is this a dagger I see before me?' But she said it was a door, and would I show the next person in?

She did give me some leaflets on my rights, but they didn't take long to read because apparently I haven't got any.

All the same, I've now got the Advice Bug and am not going to give up. The next Advisor I see I'll put on my poshest gear and accent and suck up to them like mad.

Dad's always going on about the glories of trades unionism so next I'll try the NUS.*

Student Power, now!

Yours fraternally,

Maxie

*That's the National Union of Students. I thought you might not know, seeing as you're now hanging around with anti-trade union fascists.

PS   Sorry again.

PPS   I've got geography in two hours, so wish me luck!

Dearest J,

No time like the present – this morning I skived off school to see a welfare advisor at the NUS.

I had to hide in Amanda's garden shed next door till Mum and Sue left for work and Dad slouched off to sign on. Then I snuck back home and dumped my uniform. I had to lie on the phone about being a NUS member so thought at least I should look grown up. Dress for Success, that's the thing! Sue's new suit *does* look great on me, even if she did choose the colour to match her hair, not mine. She's a mean git.

On the bus to the NUS place in Euston I felt dead nervous. I ended up catching a one-man bus on Dad's old route and I couldn't help thinking that if he still had his job I wouldn't be making this journey. In his cranky old way, Dad used to be proud of me and want me to 'get on'.

Mum says Dad's lost all pride in himself, that's the problem. I was thinking about this, watching the bus driver get more and more hot and bothered. It was really boiling today, and by Kings Cross the traffic was terrible. It was standing room only and the passengers were cranky. One lady even gave the driver an earful when he got stuck in a jam on Gray's Inn Road.

'Lady, what do you expect me to do?' he snarled. 'Fly the bloody bus?'

Then she demanded his number so she could complain about him swearing. I felt really sick. He could get the sack because of her. So I told her she'd lose it too if she was stuck in a cab all day surrounded by stinking exhaust fumes and daft bats like her. That just set her off on The Manners of Young People Today.

I legged the last bit, to get away from her. No wonder the stress drove Dad to nervous eczema and the dole. It's thanks to passengers like her that I now face a life-time as a child labourer.

And no, I didn't get much joy from the NUS. For starters, this welfare bloke was at the pub. And when I tracked him down, he and his mate were *sitting outside on the pavement!* Dead grungy they were, all matted hair and filthy jeans, and they didn't offer me a chair so I had to sit there too.

They were busy drafting some leaflet on Class and Elitism in Education, whoever he is when he's at home. They didn't even pretend to be impressed by my best Royal accent or terrible problems.

I explained that Dad was a self-made man who only believed in The University of Life. But I was a genius doing 15 GCSEs and, if only I could get a government grant to stay on at school, one day I'd be rich and famous and a super rate tax-payer like him. So really it was in the national interest to invest in me.

They said genius was 'an elitist concept', and there weren't any grants, 'even for the kids who really need them'. They obviously didn't mean me.

Maybe I should have admitted Dad was on the sick. All this trip's achieved is certain death at Sue's hands. Her suit got all mucky on the pavement and sponging's just rubbed the stains in. I've hidden it in my wardrobe but she's got a nasty suspicious mind so will probably look for it there. If you never hear from me again, you'll know why.

Yours,

The unadvisable Maxine

65

Dear Jean,

Thank you for suggesting that I think about people
worse off than me. But there aren't any.

I assume you got that gem of compassion from your
Torrid Tory.

After this wonderful week I can add physics and maths
to the list of exams I've now failed. And that's the least
of my worries. You remember Sue's suit? Tonight I smug-
gled Frankie up to my room and he got out the stains
with bike-cleaning spirit. But then the suit ponged a bit
so I hung it outside our bedroom window to air. How
was I to know that while I was in the bath, getting the
pong off *me*, there'd be a thunderstorm? Or that the suit
would blow downstairs and shrink?

Sue marched straight up to the bathroom and started
bashing down the door. I was terrified. I tried reasoning
with her through the door. I told her I'd never liked the
colour anyway and that it wouldn't hurt her to go on a
diet. But she's completely irrational. Just because her
stupid suit's now two sizes too small, she gave me a black
eye!

Actually it was the bathroom door that gave me the
shiner: it bounced off my face when Sue bust the bolt.
I was yelling, 'You can't hit me, I'm a pacifist', but she
still laid into me. It was *so* humiliating. I was starkers and
Sue was raving like a lunatic. Eventually Mum pulled Sue
off me but *she* was screaming about the damage to the

door. She didn't even notice the damage to my face. That did it. I hurled on some clothes and ran off to the Maloneys.

Frankie and Imelda couldn't have been kinder. I could hardly see, what with crying so much and my eye ballooning up, so I asked if they had any steak to stop the swelling. They only had a couple of sausages in the fridge, but Imelda taped them to my eye, while Frankie made me a cup of sweet tea, to save me, he said, from Going into Shock.

And that's when it happened, Jean – when Frankie finally let slip his love for me. He called me *Darling!* Even though I had two pink bangers sellotaped to my mush! It was really romantic.

This is the one good thing to have come out of me being an Abused Child.

Then Mrs Maloney came in and she was lovely too, considering the sausages were for Mr M's tea. 'Oh, he'll never notice the difference,' she said, once she'd wiped them clean of my eye shadow.

I wish she were my mum. She's dead against violence. If the little Maloneys are rowing she threatens them all with her rolling pin then sprinkles them with Holy Water. She's a proper mum. She even makes cakes.

Mine's so selfish she won't even pay me to do her cleaning.

Frankie was so worried for me he walked me back. We sat on Amanda's garden wall for a while, the bit round the corner so we were out of sight of the Sadists of Sheraton Road. I finally broke it to Frankie that I'm planning to move away. I sounded dead tough and told him I'd got it all planned, but he was still gob-smacked.

When he finally left me on the doorstep he sighed, 'I just wish I could protect you from the muggers indoors.'

67

Droopy Derek thinks he's marrying a real lady. I wonder when he'll realise locals know her as a vicious criminal?

Then Frankie put his hand to my cheek. It was a truly tender gesture, even if he was only wiping sausage meat from it.

'We can't got on like this,' he said, just like the heroes in those old films. 'You deserve better. Tomorrow, Max, I'll work something out – something that will really cheer you up. I promise.'

Oh, Jean – I could have fainted!

Whatever can he mean?

And how am I going to get through eight hours tomorrow of GCSE English revision?

Yours, beaten but not bowed, all soft and soggy,

Maxine 'Darling' Maloney

Saturday night
June 20th

Dearest Jean,

I'm so excited I can't keep still! Frankie's late because of that 'something special' he's organising for me. I'm scribbling to you to try and control myself.

Even the brutal environment here at the Harrison House of Horrors hasn't been able to burst my bubble. Mum's been picking on me all day, just because I'm young and in love and refused to apologise to Sue.

I'm the one with the black eye! And I've been forced to forsake revision and give Dad a hand with the door.

You'd think he'd have been too embarrassed to be seen with me at Homebase. I warned him I was walking evidence of domestic violence. But he just yelled at me for spending twenty minutes on my make-up, then dragged me out to hunt for bits and bobs of DIY.

I spent the whole time having my most romantic fantasy ever about Frankie and me. I'm *sure* he's going to take me out somewhere posh tonight.

Tell me I'm daft but I kept imagining our candlelit dinner. How ravishing I'd look in the soft light; how Frankie's fingers would disappear beneath the table and gently, oh so gently, trace 'I love you' along my thigh; how I'd nearly swoon in ecstasy, and murmur, 'I need ... I need ... fresh air ...' and Frankie would lead me tenderly into the night ...

Unfortunately, every time I got to *that* part of my fantasy, Dad would interrupt AND expect me to have found the right bit for his drill! After shaking me for the third time he got suspicious and wanted to know what I was 'mooning about'. As if I'd tell him! You know what filthy minds parents have – he'd never understand this is *true love*.

Gotta run – I've forgotten to cotton-bud my ears. Don't fellas have it easy, getting ready for a date? Tonight I've filed and polished my nails, whitened my teeth with bicarb, shaved everything bar the bath rug, moisturised my bod, tinted, gelled and blow-dried my hair, painted my face and black eye, and still Mum expects me to find the energy to tidy the bathroom. I expect that's why she's screaming at me now. But I've left it clean, I wiped up all the puddles with the towels.

Much love,

Max

Dear J,

Frankie's Something Special was to take me flat hunting. How helpful. I'd far rather have been wined and
dined.

He's worried about me Being Taken Advantage of. I
wish!

Frankie says loads of landlords are rip-off merchants,
so he spent all of yesterday racing round on Deirdre
checking out places in the ads. What he showed me last
night was the best of the bunch.

I tried to seem enthusiastic but looking at poky little
bed-sits was hardly romantic. The biggest was a ten foot
by eight foot one-room hovel. 'There's a lot you can do
with a room this size,' he said. 'Like what,' I asked,
'suffocate?' Then the landlady said Beggars Can't Be
Choosers and laughed when I pointed out that I'm a
junior marketing executive.

She didn't 'hold' with A Girl Your Age Leaving Home.
The other landladies didn't either. And Frankie didn't
hold anything except the *Evening Standard* — he was too
busy pretending to be my brother.

I know it was sweet of him, and I really was grateful,
but what a waste of war-paint.

Then my evening's highlight — yes, you've guessed it,
The Three Boring Brewers. That's where Frankie spilled
his *really* good news. He thinks I'm crazy to leave home,
but knows I'm 'headstrong'. He wants to see me 'safely
settled' because his entire family is off to Ireland for a
month and he's 'got' to go too. Just because his grandma
is dying.

He's dutiful, responsible, caring and thoughtful. And I hate him.

He's deserting me on Tuesday.

Three days before my 16th birthday.

And to think I'm now in danger of failing English for him.

I am so depressed. Can't write another word.

M.

The Prison
96 Sheraton Road
London N8

June 25th

Dear J,

HOORAY! Free at *last*! (Well, from school anyway.) CONGRATULATIONS on surviving the exams. Wasn't it great finishing with English? I even got a question about *The Merchant of Venice* and forgiveness, which was just up my street seeing as I'm such a forgiving person.

Honestly, though, I'm upset about your phonecall. I am *not* 'selfish and self-obsessed'. I know Frankie's grandma can't help dying, but she could've picked a better time.

As for saying I never ask after you, I hear all about your woes when you ring up. It's me that spends hours writing letters to keep you cheerful and put things in perspective.

But that's enough carping. I'm CELEBRATING! And more than you think. I've some brilliant news. Yes, you've guessed it – I've finally found our flat! I saw it tonight straight after whizzing through my English paper.

Actually, the flat's what the *Evening Standard* calls a 'B/sit and ck facs'. The ck facs – cooking facilities – are just one electric ring, but as we're going to get healthy and only cook Ryvita from now on, who cares? OUR OWN PLACE AT LAST!

It's in Finsbury Park and a bit dingy, but twice the size of the others I've seen. D-Day – Departure – is the end of this week. The landlady says it will take that long to clean seeing as her last tenant wasn't in a fit state to tidy up before going back to the bin. She's a very kind woman, Mrs O'Donahue. She specialises in people needing Care In The Community.

Actually, I have to confess I felt a bit nervous when she asked me whether I wanted the room. We'd only been there a second and it seemed an awfully big decision to make on the spot. (Yes, I *know* you told me so.) But I realised it was now or never. So I took one last look just to be certain – it's got lots of potential really if you ignore the mildew – and said, 'Sure, it's great. I'll take it.'

I'm sorry I didn't share the good news with you straightaway on the phone tonight but I don't have a shred of privacy in this dungeon and I don't dare let Mum and Dad know where I'm going. They're bound to tell me they won't let me do it, and I can't risk that – not after everything I've been through. So I've got no choice. I'm going to have to scarper, do a moonlit flit, take French Leave.

I'll hang in till after my birthday, though. Even *my*

mean family are bound to give me dosh for my 16th. I'll need it for the paint and plants and curtains. The flat will be really lovely when I've scrubbed off the mould and taken the nylon sheets down from the window.

As it is, the full rent's half my M & S wages *and* I was meant to cough up a month's in advance. I could only give Mrs O'Donahue half but I promised I'd pay her in full before I moved in. Since I'm sure you're feeling upset about calling me selfish, how about lending me the rest and making yourself feel better?

Don't worry if you can't send all the money you've saved from working in the bar. Every little bit helps, as the old lady said when she peed in the sea.

I'm really excited. You'd think I'd be scared but I'm not, honest. So what if the area's a little run down. I expect that means a lot of exciting Bohemian types live there. I shall be amongst My Own People at last. The artistic, sensitive kind.

Thanking you in advance,

Your loving, grateful friend Maxine

PS Frankie left an hour ago and I miss him already, though his farewell kiss was more concerned than passionate. He just couldn't stop fretting about me moving out. 'I still don't like it, Max,' he sighed, even though Mrs O'Donahue *promised* him she'd take especially good care of his sister. She thinks I'm *very* sensible and mature for an 18 year old.

PPS Don't forget I'm 16 in three days!
Post my prezzie *now*!

Dear Jean,

Thanks a million – a friend in need is a friend indeed, although I do think 50 per cent interest is a bit steep. How about 25?

Your postal order and present were the only things that stopped me from bursting into tears this morning. I'd *said* I wanted money for my birthday but Mum still went ahead and bought me her usual tasteless rubbish. God, she must think I'm twelve, getting me a Care Bears nightdress case and a 100 per cent pure gilt charm bracelet.

Then there was this revolting cheap perfume she must have got from a pavement hawker down Wood Green. It stunk of chemicals so much that I said she'd be better off using it to shift the stains off her teeth. I was on the verge of tears but she's so selfish my mum, she beat me to it.

I had a drink this evening with Rosie, the other girls from school and my drama group mates to celebrate my birthday and the new flat. It was good of them to all turn up but it ended up leaving me feeling a bit low. Everyone was excited about the exams being over and breaking up early. I'm not sure anyone even realised that I might not be back at Haringey Girls after the summer 'holidays'. (Zimbabwe for Grace, Tenerife for Anna, Portugal for Rosie, Wood Green M & S for me.)

I did get some nice prezzies, but so many goodbyes has wrung me out. Rosie isn't going to be around to help me move. She's off in the morning for a month of sun, sea and sand. Luckily, I overhead Cas telling Anna

74

that he can borrow his Mum's car whenever he likes, so I roped him in instead.

He really is lovely, Jean. He even brought me a paper daffodil tonight as a birthday gift. He's so creative – which is more than I can say about Frankie. The present he left behind for me was his unopened wage packet. I know I wanted money but he hadn't even wrapped it in a ribbon. How was I going to show *that* off to my mates?

Thank you for your interesting present, *Cooking in a Bedsit*. This will extend my culinary range – I already do a brilliant Pot Noodles.

I had a few anxious moments when I opened your parcel. Mum gave me one of her piercing 'what's-going-on' stares when I saw the title and hid it. I tried to act natural, even though I'd stuffed it up my shirt. It's hard graft keeping anything a secret in the Harrison household. But I won't have to worry about that much longer. Only twenty-four hours to Independence! I really can't wait!

Much love,

Max

Post Pot Noodles

Dear Jean,

I'm here! I figured you'd be anxious to know if my getaway was a success. It was, though it did get a bit tricky at times. It's hard to act casual when your mum keeps giving you the 'I-know-something's-up' eyeball. But I didn't crack under the pressure and am now relaxing happily in my own flat.

I have to confess, it was pretty sad packing up my stuff this morning while Dad was at his 900th job interview. I nearly cried in my room over my photos of M & D holding me when I was a baby. But that was then, this is now, and they don't love me any more. So I left the photos still pinned to the wall, the better to hurt them with. For good measure, I pinned my goodbye note to the Care Bears.

I then spent the next hour panicking that Cas wouldn't show up before Dad got back, even though I'd called him the minute the coast was clear. Luckily, he arrived in time. I didn't believe his story about bad traffic for a minute, but he's so gorgeous, I forgave him on the spot. I didn't even make a fuss about the non-stop Reggae he was blaring out of his mum's Volvo although it ruined my plans for a dead quiet getaway.

Cas plays non-stop Reggae and wears Rasta colours because he was Black in a previous incarnation. He says

76

his tight curly hair is proof, even though it's blond. He can be a dead pretentious twerp at times. He had a good laugh at Mum's zebra striped suite and said it's so Seriously Non Happening, it's no wonder I needed to Blow and get my own Yard. He reckons Finsbury Park is Well Bad and full of Cool Dudes. But he didn't stay long after dropping me off.

Getting settled on my own was a bit daunting at first. But since I've cleaned the flat I feel much better. I got rid of the green furry thing rotting in the saucepan and I've sprayed all over with deodorant. Now the whole place whiffs of lily-of-the-valley, mixed with just a tinge of old sock. (Not mine.) I'd sleep with my window open but I'm on the ground floor.

I wish I'd brought the remains of Mum's cake. She went to a lot of effort really, writing 'Sweet Sixteen' in smarties. I'd nip out for some more Pot Noodles from the late night supermarket on the corner. But I'm a bit scared to go out here after dark on my own.

Still, we'll feel better once we join Imelda's self-defence class, won't we?

You do still want to leave home, don't you?

It's really fun.

Write soon. Please.

Max

Dearest Jean,

I wouldn't normally write three letters in a row but thought I should tell you about my busy social life.

I've got to know the three other tenants here and the lady in the corner shop. I really felt part of the Community going down to buy my Nescafé, noodles and Ryvita. You know I can't stand coffee, but as I told Mrs Patel, 'You've got to have it for guests.'

Then I sat down and waited for some, and sure enough, four hours later Cas and his sister Liberty pitched up. It was mega crucial having mates pop in without Dad poking his head round the door and grunting, 'Who's this scruffy layabout?'

Actually Cas and Liberty think caffeine wires you up so they only drink herb tea. I had to admit I'd clean run out, but it's amazing how nice plain boiled water tastes. We all agreed it made a lovely change. They promised that once I've de-furred Mrs O'Donahue's kettle they'll be back for more.

They couldn't stop long, they were expected home for Sunday 'lunch' as they call it. I must admit I felt a little jealous. And sad. And hungry. My dad's a self-confessed chauvinist boar but his Sunday roasts are something else. Potatoes all crisp from the oven and crumbly soft inside, all soaked in rich gravy. And meat . . .

Not Pot Noodles. Not Ryvita. MEAT.

Oh, well. I'm sure Cas and Liberty are right and I look healthier now I've gone vegetarian.

78

I've got nowhere to store meat here anyway. Dominic, who's got the room above me, really knows the ropes. He's shown me how to use the windowsill as a fridge. It works a treat except at this time of year, when your milk and butter go rancid.

Dominic's a *painter*! He must have led a fascinating life, though when I asked about it he went all quiet and modest. He's lived most of his life abroad. He's about 40 and a perfect gentleman. Apparently, I remind him of his daughter. He hasn't seen her since she was two but his room's stuffed with pictures of what he thinks she must look like now.

Then there's ancient Miss Z, who's got some unpronounceable name so everyone calls her Your Highness. Her room's all chintzy and neat except for the cans she's recycling to finance the restoration of the Polish monarchy. She's sweet but a bit barmy. She says Aaron, the man in number 4, poisoned her nobleman father.

Dominic reckons she's just cross because Aaron never gives her any cans. He says Aaron's no trouble except when he forgets to take his medicine. I wanted to ask Aaron if he was feeling better when we met outside the toilet, but he ran away. It must be awful to be shy.

Dominic's taught me how to stick up my posters using toothpaste. I've got a cute Greenpeace photo of a seal that Rosie gave me as a housewarming-birthday present, plus posters of my fave bands, but I guess my room still looks a bit soulless.

There's a huge double bed, a lumpy eiderdown, an enormous wardrobe that hogs half the space, and the 'kitchen area' is an earthenware sink. I haven't had the chance to do any painting yet because of all my socialising. Perhaps I should wait for you and we could chose a colour scheme together?

My matching duvet set would also help. I wonder if Mum and Dad would mind me taking it? I did think of ringing today but I don't suppose they've even realised I'm missing. Besides, I couldn't find a phone-box that works.

Gotta go – tomorrow I start at Marks. I'm a little nervous but how hard can it be? If only the uniform wasn't so ghastly, I'd be a bit more enthusiastic. Still, I've got discount knickers to look forward to.

Hope you're not jealous I'm having such a great time.

Love,

Max

PS   What exactly do vegetarians eat? Apart from baked beans I mean?
PPS   We can share the bed when you come if you like as there isn't room for another one. But I know you're into healthy living, so perhaps you'd prefer the floor? It'd be dead good for your back.

Finsbury Park
July 3rd

Dear Jean,

Thank you for your postcard, '100 Years of First Aid'. You're either psychic or sick. Being battered isn't a joke.

On Monday when I got to Marks, Dad was waiting on the pavement and almost lynched me. He screamed that Mum had aged ten years overnight. She'd rung the police but they said there was nothing they could do. Then she'd rung all my mates but they either didn't know or wouldn't say where I was. I was mortified, standing being yelled at in the middle of the street, but Dad kept on shouting and hollering.

'You and your posh bloody acting friends'. 'What in hell do you think you were doing?' 'Don't you have any brains at all?'

Oh Jean, why did you have to pick this weekend to go away? You could have told them where I'd gone. It would have saved me a lot of embarrassment *and* put my mum out of her misery.

I'd have done it myself, but I didn't realise she was in any.

Dad really showed me up in front of all the other girls. If he'd wanted to have a go he could have made an appointment for lunch or something. So much for making a good impression on my first day. I'd been really determined not to let on that I was a school-leaver and that this was my first full-time job. But it's hard to seem cool when you've been treated in public like a 16-year-old.

I know I *am* 16 but that's not the point.

I did feel guilty, though, when I saw Mum. Dad made me go round after work and she looked awful, all shrivelled up and wrinkled. She was still in her dressing-gown and stinking of fags.

It was so strange going back and thinking, 'I lived here once'.

Mum ranted on hysterically about runaways ending up raped and murdered. I pointed out that that would save her the cost of feeding me. I meant it as a joke to calm her down but then she flipped completely. First she smashed me across the face, a real whopper, and the next minute she was cuddling and kissing me and sobbing that she'd kill anyone who dared lay a finger on her baby.

I *ask* you, aren't parents irrational?

To cut a long story short, M & D came back with me to inspect my flat. I was dead scared Mrs O'Donahue would come out and ask after my brother. Fortunately we were only spotted by Miss Z, who was an angel. She told them I was a lovely, well brought up girl. I think she added 'for a peasant' but her accent's so thick they didn't spot it.

M & D weren't too thrilled by the room, or the house, or the area. But after whispering in the corner they agreed that a little self-sufficiency might Do Me Good, teach me The Value of Money, yawn, yawn, yawn. As long as I stayed in touch and told them what I was doing, they'd respect my decision.

Then Mum slipped me a tenner and told me to buy a phone card. Brilliant! Now I've half the cost of this skirt I was lusting after.

Even though I'm cream crackered after eight hours of learning how to fend off deranged customers demanding refunds on 2-year-old, sweat-stained bras, I feel okay really. I told the girls at Marks who saw Dad shouting at me that he was a local nutter I'd once made the mistake of befriending. My supervisor, Hatchet Face Hartley, wasn't very sympathetic when my upset at his fit made me count out the wrong change three times, but otherwise I made a brilliant impression on my first day at work.

It's really great being independent of your parents and a carefree career girl. Do try it sometime.

Soon.

I miss you.

Love,

Maxine

PS   I don't want to pressure you but Mum thinks you're moving in with me next week.

July 5th
10 pm, After Rehearsals

Dear Jean,

Thank you for your food parcel. Next time, could you send the crisps in their packets? I really don't think the police are going to intercept my mail, trace the packets back to your dad's wine bar, and then do me for Receiving Stolen Goods. Even if they did, I really wouldn't care. At least in prison you get fed.

I know after the exams I wanted my thunder thighs tamed, but I didn't aim on starving them into submission. I'm just a reformed chocaholic, not some royal anorexic. I *hate* being hungry.

I was so excited opening your parcel most of the crisps fell straight onto the floor. But I did manage to cobble together one decent crisp sandwich. At tonight's rehearsal I told Cas what I'd had for tea. I thought he'd be dead impressed by my new minimalist vegetarian diet. But he just creased up and said, 'If it's true what they say – "You are what you eat" – you might as well give up, Max!' Then he started calling me Salt and Vinegar.

I was so upset I'd have forgotten my lines if I had any. Instead I got all my movements wrong, pushed when I was supposed to squeeze and slithered when I was meant to crawl. Being in a daft play is bad enough, but being bad in a daft play really is the pits.

Amanda gave me a right rollicking. She said I wasn't

even trying. But how do you act out 'the stillness of the womb' when your stomach's rumbling like a cistern? I'll bet Vanessa Redgrave never had this problem. It's all very well her being a Revolutionary actress. She only knows about Deprivation from books. I, Jean, am the Real Thing.

Afterwards the group went to the pub. I made some excuse, hoping they'd guess I was broke and needed a sub. But no one did.

It was buying that skirt that did it. Until I'm paid next week, I'm brassic.

So there I was, all dressed up with nowhere to go. God knows why but I decided to cheer my family up by popping in. Well, Friday night in front of the telly must get boring.

I really wanted to catch up on my soaps but Dad said as he pays the licence he was keeping the sport on. Mum and Sue were poring over some wedding catalogue, so they weren't bothered.

And they'd finished their tea.

Mum did give me a couple of towels, so I can stop using the tea towel here to dry myself. But I can't say the Prodigal Daughter's first visit home thrilled them much.

I've been re-reading *Catcher in the Rye*, which is quite uplifting. I cried at that bit where Holden Caulfield runs away from school, but only because I was thinking about all the *really* homeless kids nowadays, the ones sleeping in doorways.

I know I won't end up like that because, whatever Mum and Dad think, I *am* learning to budget. I've had a real brainwave. My shampoo's finished but in future I'll wash my hair with Fairy Liquid.

Neat, huh? And I'm not really miserable. But please please please write soon. And tell me when you're coming.

Kisses,

Max

July 7th
Midnight

Dearest Jean,

Fab night! I was just getting ready to spend Sunday evening washing my uniform's armpits when Cas and Liberty came round and invited me to a *rave*! They said I could pay Jonathan back for the ticket later (he's ill and couldn't go.)

It was really great, even if I wasn't looking my best. The good thing about washing your hair in Fairy Liquid is that you don't need gel afterwards, it's stiff anyway. So that's another couple of quid I'll save.

Liberty was a bit snotty about my 'image'. I *did* feel a little out of place. Most of the other kids were in hippy gear, and there was me in my new teeny weeny mini skirt and scuffed white high heels. But once I realised everyone was too into their own thing to pay attention to me, I felt fine. I kicked off my shoes and felt a right rebel.

It was magic — after a while I was dancing really well. I felt as if the music was sliding inside my skin. I *was* the sounds. I stopped caring about my clothes and I'm sure Cas was seeing me differently – not as a mate but a *girl*.

Frankie's never danced with me the way Cas did tonight. Cas only touched me occasionally, like it was accidental or because the crowd was packed so tight, but then when his hand ran down my back – oh, Jean! Talk about melting. I'm surprised I didn't have to be carried home in a bucket!

But then – wait for it! – Cas invited me out! He wants me to go to Brighton with him next Sunday!

I don't *think* this is a date – and I don't want it to be, because I love Frankie. But if Cas *does* fancy me too, will it survive the swimsuit test? Brighton means beaches means baring my bod – and my pathetic toothpaste-coloured legs.

I am now in complete despair.

I really hate my body. It isn't even fit to be donated to science.

Help!

Love,

Maxine Harrison

July 11th

Dear Jean,

OK, OK, I can quite understand why that Conservatives' party has put you off sex 'n booze. I'm sorry you had to get legless and nearly go too far in order to finally realise I'm right. Jake's sordid, not suave.

But please spare me the lectures about becoming a drug fiend, just because I went to a rave. Unlike you, I *know* a girl should stay in control – especially of her bra straps.

Poor you: why don't you send your bra to the Tories' HQ with a bill for new elastic? That should terminate Jake's chances of becoming Prime Minister.

Far be it from me to say I told you so, but if you take up with Tories what can you expect? There's only about 20 in Lancashire so they're bound to be inbred and deranged.

As for him calling you 'just a barmaid', who should be 'grateful' he even bothered with you – grrr! If I weren't so broke I'd get on the first coach Oop North and wipe the smarmy grin straight off his rich git's face.

Which brings me to my main point. You're now boy-friendless and I'm skint, so what's to stop you heading South and sharing the rent? I do appreciate the crisps you keep sending me, Jean, but a few mashed packets of Golden Wonder hardly count as a flat-share.

My landlady knows all about my big sister in Ashton-under-Lyne, so as long as you're dead quiet climbing in the window at night there should be no problem.

I hate to get heavy with my best friend, but I expect your DEFINITE DATE OF ARRIVAL by the next post, or else!

With fondest wishes,

Red Max

PS Thanks for the tip about the fake sun tan cream. Unlike you I can't afford Clarins. But I'll find something.

Watch out you bronzed Brighton beach bums, here I come!

Max's Miraculous Beauty Salon

Saturday
Midnight

Dearest J,

Sorry I've got this paper greasy but it was in a good cause. You'd go green if you could see me sheen! I've emptied half a bottle of Insteda Sun all over my little white bod and now look so gorgeous I feel delirious.

I skipped rehearsals so I could start greasing up as soon as I left work. It says to re-apply after two hours for a deeper tan, and I've just finished bunging on my fourth.

But God, this fake tanning is hard work, isn't it? I hated all that scrubbing your limbs first to get rid of the dead skin. The directions said to 'exfoliate' with a 'body brush' but I had to make do with a brillo pad.

You need to feed the meter a quid here to get a decent bath, so I ended up climbing into my sink and using cold water instead. What we females do for beauty!

Then I got a crick in my arm from stretching to get the tan stuff onto my back. I don't *think* I missed my shoulder blades but I did get into a swoony fantasy about being on the beach tomorrow with Cas and having him oil my back, just like in the ads. I never realised that people get boyfriends just so they don't have to become muscle contortionists on the beach.

Of course I don't think of Cas as a boyfriend. But why should I stay loyal to Frankie? All he's sent me so far from Ireland is a Mass Card from his Nan's funeral. I'm very sorry she's dead and all that, but seeing as I've never met her, getting a picture of her now she's gone hardly counts as a love letter, does it?

But enough about me. I am gob-smacked that you've finally plucked up the courage to leave home and move in with me. We'll have a ball. I promise! Pot Noodles every night! Now that I've got thinner, I'll even be able to borrow your clothes.

I've been thinking about Patch. I agree, he is the only person in your family that understands you, but no, you can't bring him. He'd bark and pee and give you away.

Once we've got you a job we'll be able to afford a proper two-bedroomed flat, and then he can stay.

Can you bring a few other bits and pieces with you as well as Bob the Dog's camping mattress? (Ok, if you blow it up for me, I'll take turns sleeping on it too.) Your mum doesn't really need two microwaves, one downstairs in the wine bar is enough. I really don't miss anything about living with my family except bathroom scales, a full-length mirror and the telly.

So see what you can sneak out?

Roll on July 20th . . . one more week and you'll be here!

And roll on 1 am . . . then I can give myself one final going over with Insteda Sun, and get my beauty sleep!

Much love,

Maxine

Sunday July 14th

Dearest J,

First the good news. Sitting on my bed is a sweet fluffy teddy bear Cas won for me on the pier.

Now the bad news. Cas chose it specially 'to match my skin'. It's orange.

I got up at five because I hate rushing and he was due at nine. In fact it took me until eleven, when he actually turned up, to get ready. In daylight my tan looked different but I checked the colour against a tin of baked beans and it was definitely brown in comparison.

I was feeling pretty good when Cas arrived, just a bit nervous about how I'd explain my sudden tan. Being a Green he's got a thing about girls 'looking natural'. I'm not sure if he swallowed my line about skiving off Marks yesterday to sun myself. 'I thought the only thing you skived off,' he said, 'is rehearsals. And yesterday it was raining.'

I felt more relaxed, though, once we hit the road. It was a lovely hot day. We opened all the car windows and Cas played Reggae at full blast. It was just like in a road movie, with my man at the wheel and the wind tugging at my hair.

Cas really knows how to treat a girl. He spent loads of money on me at the pier, and didn't mind going on the helter skelter five times after I told him I needed to conquer my fear of heights. Really it was because I liked sitting between his legs with him holding onto me.

Then we went to the shooting range and Cas won the teddy bear for me. I was just thinking how manly and romantic he was when he made that horrible joke. By the time we went down to the beach I was feeling a bit scared about him seeing me in my swimsuit.

I already had it on underneath so I made us sit right by the water's edge, pulled off my dress and ran straight in. Brighton beach is all pebbles and it's hard to run over jagged stones and suck in your tummy at the same time. But terror makes you fast. The tide was out but I flung myself down and started swimming when it reached my knees.

I was happily doing breast stroke and ignoring the rocks scraping my tummy when Cas caught up and yanked me up. If there'd been more water he'd have drowned, he was laughing so much.

'Yo, sister, what a fraud!' he giggled, and scooped up some sand and started rubbing it on my back.

It was my shoulder blades, of course. The parts that one-armed Insteda Sun can't reach. The give-away white patches with the odd spot of orange. Since I got home, Jean, I have inspected my back in Her Highness's wardrobe mirror, and have to admit Cas was cruel but accurate.

I look like a moulting leopard.

I felt pretty awful by the time we got back to London. And I was starving. (Cas wouldn't let me 'poison' myself with seaside junk food, even though I'd have killed for a chip.) So I asked him to drop me at Mum and Dad's, in case they were worried about wasting the left-overs from their Sunday dinner. That's when he turned off the engine and went all quiet.

I thought maybe, despite me being orange, he could see through to the real me, and was plucking up the courage for a kiss. I realised that underneath he was sensitive too. So I snuggled up closer to make it easier for him and said, 'You're really sweet when you're shy.'

'You'd feel shy too, Max,' he muttered, 'if you had to tell someone they've been dropped from the group.'

I didn't take it in at first. It was only when he mumbled he'd taken me out to cheer me up that I realised *I'd* been dropped.

Cas said it's because I've missed so many rehearsals recently. Amanda thinks I've got 'too much on my plate'.

But there was nothing on my plate tonight. After Cas roared off, I realised I couldn't face Mum and Dad. I've told them it's worth educating me because one day I'll take the stage by storm. But I can't even keep a part in a poxy little theatre group.

I felt like chucking a brick through Amanda's window. But I didn't want her to see me crying. So I just walked home – all four miles to Finsbury Park. At least it was dark by then, so I wasn't in any danger of people laughing at my skin. Just of being molested by men with no taste.

I forgot to tell you – there's a red light district a couple of roads down from the bed-sit. Walk up there on your own at night and it doesn't matter what you look like, some creepy kerb-crawler will still ask, 'How much?'

There's nothing worse than having to snarl 'Sod off!' to some man with money when you haven't even got your bus fare home.

Actually, there is one thing worse. It's walking the streets and seeing the bluey flicker of television screens behind net curtains, and people coming in and out of rooms, and knowing there's some family settling down with a cuppa for a nice night together with a good weepy film.

And knowing that you don't have a real home, or a family.

Dear Jean, please come soon, don't let me down.

I don't like to admit this, but sometimes I get lonely. Yours, about to scrub my skin raw so I can face Marks tomorrow,

Maxine

27 Whitehorn St,
NOT in N7's Red Light District

July 17th

Dearest J,

Thank you for your cheering letter. But please stop freaking out about moving into a red light district. There's only *one* road near by that's bad and, if you're young, hip and streetwise, coping's no bother. You just take a half-mile detour to miss it.

Are you *sure* you've told your Mum and Dad you're leaving for good? Telling me you'll 'see how things go' in London is selfish. Either you're dying to live with me or you're not.

I'm sorry to sound harsh, but if your best friend can't break it to you that you're in danger of becoming a wimp, who can?

THINK POSITIVE!

I'm in such a good mood because I went home tonight and M and D were (for once) really nice to me. They must miss me a lot, which I suppose is only natural. Even Sue was quite civilised, once she realised I was an extra pair of hands for her pre-marital cook-in. She's cooking all her wedding grub in advance, because Amanda next door (yes, that witch) is letting her store it in her freezer.

Sue has talked Mum out of a spam sandwich buffet (her idea, poor thing, of pushing the boat out) and into going posh. They're going to have little pastry things stuffed with prawns and *quiches*!

Of course I didn't mind helping out because Mum let me stuff my face with the vol-au-vent mixture whenever Sue went out of the kitchen. We were such a merry little bunch, laughing because we were crying from the onions, that I quite forgot that I hate them.

Sue did start to create when she caught Mum slipping me one of the quiches to take home with me. I shut her up by pointing out that it's good luck to give to the poor before you marry, so she'd better give me two or she'd end up divorced.

Sue isn't kind but she is superstitious. She even gave me a couple of tins of prawns when I mentioned that meanness makes you sterile. Sue is set on producing two mini-Dereks as soon as she's spliced. I'd have thought that just *looking* at Derek would make any sensible female's ovaries curdle in self-defence. But poor Sue thinks the world is lacking in people with no chins.

She's sick of working at that snooty boutique Ravers. I can understand that, now that I too am a full-time shop worker (well, I would be, if Marks hadn't ordered bed-rest till I'm over my jaundice). But as I said to Mum, some of us see education, not babies, as the way out of shop work.

'Oh don't start, Max,' said Mum, 'we've had such a nice night.'

I told her I couldn't believe this was the same woman who used to keep me up at night while she drank her Spanish gut-rot, and cried about missing her chances so I had to have mine.

'That was before they started making students take out loans,' she said. 'People like us can't take risks. And I don't want you hurt, Max, trying for something you can't get.'

Then (and I could hardly believe this, because my mother *never* admits she's wrong), she asked me to come home! Well – she asked whether coping on my own had taught me any lessons yet, which I guess was her way of begging me.

I would have said Yes! there and then, except:

YOU! are arriving in three days' time.

Still, I wanted to leave Mum with some shreds of pride so I told her my sad experience using Fairy Liquid on my hair. Then, to make her feel better about herself, I let her lend me some Omo and shampoo.

Poor woman. She's obviously forgotten that soon YOU! will be here, and my rave-a-minute single girl life will begin in earnest!

I can't wait!

See you soon, tons of love,

Max

95

Jean.

I am writing this two hours after your mother's descent on Finsbury Park, and your departure. I can hardly see the paper because my eyes are like golfballs from crying.

Next time you leave home, kindly have the maturity to tell your mother where you're going. Pretending you were going to stay at *my parents' house, with me there*, was plain stupid. You might have guessed she would ring to remind you to brush your teeth. And get my dad saying, 'You want Jean? Which one of my good-for-nothing daughter's friends is she?'

(Pretending he can't remember my friends' names, or even mine, is just one of the little mannerisms that drove me out from under his roof.)

You might have known that your mother would then hot-foot it down to London to 'rescue' you, as she so dramatically put it. You might even have guessed, from what I told you about the streets round here, that a kerb-crawler with a fetish for middle-aged bottle blondes would follow your mother to the door.

I am only glad that Her Highness opened it and dealt with him. If an 81-year-old deposed aristocrat can frighten off a ruffian serf, why can't your mother?

Wimpishness must run in your family.

I am deeply hurt that your mother now has such a low opinion of me. I noted that you said not one word in my defence. If I didn't know you better, I could almost imagine you were *glad* to be 'rescued'.

I know not everything went as we planned, but we had some good times, didn't we?

I'm sorry that Dominic upstairs decided you were his long-lost daughter, and sang lullabies all night outside our door. Like he said in the morning, it was just the drink talking.

He's really quite harmless, even if he never did live abroad but was in the bin. Or prison. As he told your mum, when he was grovelling about not sending her maintenance all these years, it was only for things like credit card fraud, so he could buy paint. He'd never hurt anyone, especially not his own daughter.

Dominic is one of SOCIETY'S VICTIMS, Jean – just like me. For all you know, you were sharing a house with the next Vincent Van Gogh. If Dominic in despair posts his ear through my door, I shall know who to blame.

And I am *not* 'slovenly'. You know perfectly well I was only saving the cans till I had time to wash them out for Miss Z. Even if I am a Republican, I enjoy making her happy. I have a naturally generous nature.

Finally – and despite what your mother said when she saw our Pot Noodle pots – we did do quite well for fresh vegetables. We had baked beans, didn't we? Oh, well, there's no point me getting at you. For all I know, you might really *want* to be a barmaid.

Yours, alone but unbowed,

M

July 26th

Dear Jean,

I'll ignore the ranting bits in your letter. I'll put them down to your Culture Shock after being abruptly moved back to the nerdish North.

I appreciated your apology though.

All right, I'm sorry too.

It's rotten, your mother grounding you for a month. But as Ashton-Under-Slime is so boring, do you really mind?

Please could you use Australian stamps on your letters in future? Dominic has asked me for your address, so he can claim Child Benefit for you. I told him you'd emigrated.

I'm coping fine. I've only got £1 left till pay day, but I've still got a tin of sardines, five Ryvitas, and four past-their-sell-by-date yoghurts Mr Habib asked me to take off his hands. He also kindly told me that if I were his daughter he would beat me: he is scandalised that I have left home. I said I'd had to, to escape the local chocolate pushers. I meant it as a joke but he looked quite hurt.

Also Mum fed me tonight. I was just walking by Bert's and fortunately on my third time past she spotted me. I had some lovely fat juicy chips and a huge cod, two helpings of mushy peas, a pickled egg, the lot.

Mum even gave me some of those little packets of Tartare sauce to take home. If I mix them up with my sardines tomorrow night, I can imagine I'm eating somewhere fancy. Sue says posh places always drown your food in sauce.

Mum says why don't I use my staff discount to buy food at Marks. But it's mostly fancy foreign stuff and even at half price pricey. And do you remember how many 50ps it took to defrost their pre-baked potatoes in my Baby Belling?

I still think M & D are monsters, but they're right about the cost of living.

What worries me, Jean, is if I can't even afford basics when I'm working full time, how will I cope when I'm back at school and just have weekend earnings?

Mum waited with me at the bus stop tonight and got a bit tearful. Since your mum stormed down she's been trying to talk to Dad about me, school and everything. But she hasn't got anywhere. She said she could have died of shame when your mum came round, all concerned about us, and Dad said complacently that living on my own would 'toughen me up'. Toughen me? If I was shoe leather I'd never wear out!

Dominic has let me borrow his radio because he's painting and I've been listening to this late night talk show. There was this snotty-voiced Tory on, saying how The Family was the solution to kids sleeping in shop doorways. I was so angry. If it had been my radio I'd have kicked it. What about Suzy? She's new at Marks and Sparks, 17 and also away from home. She told me yesterday when we were in the stockroom that her old man once beat her so hard he broke her jaw.

The hospital was suspicious but she was frightened to tell the truth.

She did ring a helpline twice, but all she got was a tape-recorded message saying, Sorry, The Lines Are Busy.

She was 13 and had a mouth full of wire.

She's dead tough, Suzy, hard as nails. She's living with a bloke now. She says he's a pig really, always going off with other girls, but she sort of loves him and what else can she do? She says it's better than the children's home she'd ended up in, where everyone was on drugs. And that was just the staff!

Then we got told off for spending so long looking for more 36Ds and had to go back onto the floor. But I felt sad and angry all afternoon. I can't bear those smug Family Values types going on about how people in trouble have to 'help themselves'. How can you, when everything is against you?

Maybe that's how Dad feels. Tonight I even felt sorry for him. Mum says he's just had another rejection letter. She says when you're his age and have been off sick for months nobody wants to know.

He's so ashamed, he's even stopped going to his precious union.

Please write soon.

I'm sorry for calling you a wimp.

With much love,

Maxine

100

Flat 1,
The Hot Hip City
Finsbury Park, N7

August 2nd

Dear Jean,

Tonight I'm feeling very sophisticated. I have been invited to Suzy's party! There'll be loads of real *men* there – well past the pimples and bum fluff stage.

This evening when we were leaving work I noticed Suzy giving me the once-over. Then she said, 'You don't really look just 16,' and asked if I was free for her and Wayne's flat-warming tomorrow.

It was great to be able instantly to say 'Yes'. No bother about getting M & D's permission, being interrogated about what time I'd be back or *how* I'd get back, boring stuff like that. Oh, the glamour of Independence!

Then I realised only nerds are free on Saturday night so I pretended I'd need to check with mates I'd planned to go clubbing with.

'Oh, they can come too,' she said, 'as long as they're not the Doc Martens brigade.' Then she was off running for her bus, yelling 'Remember – sexy, trendy types only!'

That left me in panic. I'd got nothing sexy to wear and no mates to bring. What with working and moving away and no phone, I've lost touch with most people. So I blew as much as I dared of my wages in one of those late-night Cypriot dress wholesalers at Finsbury Park. Then I rang Rosie and told her to ring round everyone who's half cool.

The dress is great. One of those tube things, dead

short, dead black, dead clingy. I'd have been too fat for it a few months ago but now I can't afford to eat there's not that much of me to cling to.

God knows Suzy could do with a party after all she's been through. She told me today that Wayne's been dead nice recently and she loves him madly after all. She thinks it's probably her fault he sometimes flies off the handle. And she blames The Hairy Feminists, for making modern men feel insecure.

I didn't tell her I think I might be one. I'd better end now and get on with shaving my legs, so no one tomorrow guesses!

Wayne's 24, and most of his friends are older men too and telephone engineers like him.

I don't mean to make you jealous – I'm sure some of the school boys you meet in Ashton-under-Lyne are really sweet.

Lots of love,

Max the Cool and Trendy

Sunday

Dearest Jean,

Last night was the worst night of my life.

I felt so happy when I was making myself up in my flat, I thought I looked great. Then I took the tube to Suzy's. No matter how I pulled at it my skirt kept riding up, while a bunch of lads opposite sniggered and got biological.

I felt better once I got to Suzy's. Her boyfriend Wayne called his mates over to say hullo and they all seemed very admiring. One, Dean, said I was a right little gift-wrapped stunner too. I danced with loads and I'm sure Jason, who kept muttering about untangling my wires, was on the point of asking me for a date. But then Rosie turned up with loads of girls from school. I know I invited them but they didn't have to ruin everything by actually turning up!

These blokes seemed dead impressed by the 'classy types' from Haringey Girls and were suddenly swarming all over them.

I was just another of Suzy's shop assistant mates.

The girls had all been away and had tans to flaunt, *and* flash clothes and futures. They were all rabbiting on about going on to A Levels, then university. I even caught Muck Mouth Michelle boasting to Jason about her 'planned career in medicine'. She's thicker than a Sumo wrestler and twice as nasty, but because she looks the part, guys take her seriously.

Rosie didn't mean to rub it in but she did. She was bubbling over because her parents are letting her have a party on the day our exam results are due. They're that sure she'll do well.

I don't think my parents even know what day that is.

Then Michelle beckoned me over with her finger. 'Settle a debate for us, Max,' she ordered. 'Jason here,' – the hunk I'd been dancing with, who was now all over *her* – 'thinks girls who flash everything are cheap.' She slowly looked me up and down. 'You dress far more . . . *courageously* than I'd dare – so what do you think?'

I said Jason should ask her fiancé's opinion, and then fled for the kitchen.

I felt about two inches tall. If only I had been – my

dress might have fitted me then. Really I should have gone home. But to tell the truth I couldn't face another Saturday night in the bed-sit on my own with only a soon-to-be-clobbered seal for company. So I hid myself and my pathetic tarty dress behind the drinks table.

The next thing I knew I was drunk. It was nearly midnight, the girls from school had cleared off and in the front room people weren't dancing any more but lying on the floor in huddles. A bloke I'd been chatting to in the kitchen tried to grab me and said I was a 'tight bitch' when I told him to get lost. I started to get scared. Scared of catching the last tube home on my own, dressed like that, and scared because I wasn't sure I could afford a mini-cab.

I waded through the bodies and found Wayne, Suzy's boyfriend. He said a cab back at that time of night would cost at least a tenner. I'd only got a fiver. I asked, nervously, if Suzy could lend me the rest till Monday. But he said she'd already stomped off to bed, 'in another of her strops'.

Was it my fault, Jean, for trusting Wayne? Suzy'd told me he's got a roving eye, but I thought, surely not for girls she knows, not her *friends*? When I said I'd tube it, Wayne seemed so nice, so concerned. There were too many madmen around, he said, he wouldn't dream of letting me take that risk. *He'd* drive me home.

Maybe, for all I know, it's an old tactic – 'Here, little girlie, let me protect you from the *other* men.' Then in they go.

He was dead nice in the car, all sympathetic about my problems at home. Then when we arrived he said, 'I'm drunker than I realised. I don't want to get nicked on my way back. How about a coffee to sober me up?'

Later he said it was my fault, that everyone knows

asking for coffee is asking for sex and I'd led him on by agreeing.

Actually, I was thinking it would be nice to finally *use* that coffee I'd bought for all the guests I haven't had.

Jean, he lunged the minute I closed the door. The worst thing is, at first I let him kiss me. I shouldn't have, as Suzy's a mate, but – well, he did kiss nicely, and I was feeling awful. He made me forget about feeling stupid in my dress, and about Frankie and my family deserting me. He made me feel *wanted*.

I even found myself wondering if he'd had one row too many with Suzy and now wanted to go out with me. He'd kept saying in the car how he really admired me for having ambitions.

But that's not the way he was thinking at all. Suddenly he'd pushed me on to the bed and was lying on top of me. I *was* a bit turned on, I admit. But then he yanked up my dress and I got scared and asked him to stop. Jean, he just laughed and said he knew I didn't mean it. I told him I was a virgin but he didn't believe that either. Finally, I threatened to scream. I would've been dead embarrassed if Dominic or Her Highness had had to rescue me, but Wayne didn't know that – he was off me like a shot.

'Brilliant,' he said, 'you really pick your moments. If you're so bloody green, why do you live on your own and dress like a slut?'

Oh, Jean, it really hurts and humiliates me, just telling you about it. I've let Frankie down, Mum, myself. And I don't know how I'll look Suzy in the eye at work on Monday. I made Wayne promise he wouldn't say anything to her and he just laughed, 'I'll have forgotten your name by the time I'm home. By the way – what *is* your name?'

How could I have let a man I don't even know go so far?

I've spent all day cleaning the bed-sit. I cut up That Dress and used it for rags. I've even scrubbed the Baby Belling. But I still feel dirty.

I wish I was fourteen again, when we were kids, and the most we worried about was a boy getting to Number Two.

Please write immediately, Jean. I miss you, I need you.

Love,

Maxine

August 7th

Dearest Jean,

I'm so relieved you're still grounded and have time to reply by return of post. It's been hell on wheels here, but your long, thoughtful letter really helped.

You're very wise considering you're only ten months older than me and live in a Northern backwater. You're right, Suzy's boyfriend *did* take advantage.

You were wisest of all about me confusing that temporary sexy feeling with needing somebody to care for me. It *is* easier nowadays to talk about fancying someone than admit you just feel alone.

Next time I let a bloke anywhere near me I'll be in a yashmak. And I'll make damn sure he really likes me, and I like and trust him, before we so much as hold hands.

Come back, Frigid Frankie – all is forgiven! I've decided that maybe the Victorians were right and slow courtships are the answer after all.

They've got to be more romantic, as well as safer.

The scary thing about Saturday night was that for a few mad moments my body took over my brain. I've only just realised, Jean – I could have ended up pregnant. And by a complete dork!

I've decided that when and if I ever get round to doing It, I'll have been to my nearest Family Planning place first and emptied it of every contraceptive going. I know in steamy films no fella ever says at the bedroom door, 'Are you fixed up, darling?' or 'Do you want me to pop out to the chemist?'. But when I'm starring in films, I'll insist my contracts stipulate pre-screening ads for condoms. 'Forget buying her an ice cream, fellas – off with you to the gents. Get her something that *won't* melt in her hands!'

Now I don't feel so much cross at me as at *him*. I only wish Suzy could see it that way. He's hurt her and hurt me but it's us who are left fighting. God knows what he told her or why (to humiliate her too, I suppose), but work on Monday was awful.

Me and Suzy were straightaway made to work together, her pushing the stock trolley while I put out the new bras. I tried to chat like normal but she wouldn't talk to me at all.

And if looks could kill, I'd be writing this from a mortuary.

I decided to try and clear the air at lunch-time, but when I went up to the canteen she was already there with some other girls who'd been at the party. I went to join them but they all turned away.

'Something smells,' one of them said.

'Yeah – like a *bike*,' said another.

It was horrible. Suzy must have told them what happened. Not what *really* happened, but whatever line Wayne had spun her.

No wonder Mum says it's still a man's world, when even a lech who isn't there can turn girls against each other.

Not that I could see it like that then. I still felt too ashamed.

I ended up sitting with some older women. But they didn't really want me either. The way Suzy's bunch smirked when the wrinklies moved off, leaving me in the middle of the canteen on my own, was just too much to bear.

So I ran away. I went out the staff door and sat on the green by the tube station, with all the drunks. I did *mean* to go back, but when it got to three, when my lunch break ends, I just couldn't face it.

I've got a confession to make, Jean. It's Wednesday and I still haven't gone back. Or rung in. I should have let Marks know my jaundice has struck me down again but I'm so depressed I don't even feel up to telling a porky.

It's terrible when your belief in yourself is shattered.

Your kind letter has restored my confidence. A bit. So I'll re-appear tomorrow and pray I can brazen my way through.

But what if it doesn't work? Marks is so strict. What if I get the sack?

Please cross all your fingers for me.

Your terrified friend,

Maxie

108

August 8th

Dearest Jean,

Now I really can't go much lower. Tonight I walked
into a pizza place, stuffed my face and tried to leave
without paying.

The bill came to £1.50 more than I had. It was the
side salad that did it. I thought it came free.

I, who sometimes dream of giving up stage and screen
stardom to become a Social Worker, have instead
descended into the Criminal Classes.

I know that with my parlous finances I shouldn't have
been eating out. But I couldn't face eating in. (My food
cupboard currently contains one jar of hardly touched
coffee and three Ryvitas.) I passed this restaurant on my
way back to the bed-sit, smelt this wonderful warm
cheesy dough and just couldn't resist.

Post pizza, when I recounted my money and realised
I hadn't got enough, I wanted to die.

Legging it seemed the only solution.

I headed for the exit, dead natural except for looking
all around me, and I would have made it except for the
girl on the till at the door. When she said, 'Excuse me,
Miss', I knew I had no option but to put Plan B into
operation and pretend to have an epileptic fit.

I once helped a customer who had one in Marks, so
I knew what to do. I was so terrified I started twitching
naturally anyway.

If I wasn't so ashamed of myself I'd feel dead proud.

It really was an Oscar-winning performance. I even made my eyes go all glazed and squinty, and (this is what makes me really ashamed) the girl couldn't have been nicer. When I started to drool and mumbled I'd forgotten my pills, she shot out from behind the till, made me lie on the floor and hot-footed it for the manager. That, of course, is when I made an instant recovery and hot-footed it too.

I didn't stop running until I reached home.

Now I'm never in my life going to be able to set foot again in Seven Sisters Road. The worst thing, Jean, is knowing that I have destroyed that girl's faith in human nature. Next time a customer comes over faint, she won't call an ambulance but a Black Maria.

I know what you'll be thinking – why don't I go back after pay day and give them the dosh? Well, Jean, I can't, because I no longer have an income. Yes – Marks have sacked me.

I was eating to forget.

So much for brazening it out. When I went in today, I hid amongst the bras and hoped if I sold loads no one would bother asking where I'd been for three days. But Hatchet Faced Hartley, my cow of a supervisor, spotted me skulking amongst the camisoles and pounced.

'I don't want to hear your excuses,' she snapped, when I explained about being a registered jaundice sufferer. 'Try them on Personnel.'

It was like going to your own execution, Jean, walking off the sales floor with Suzy and all her mates sniggering. Desperately hoping that the Personnel lady would have read up on jaundice and know how awful it is for a victim like me.

Even though I was very convincing, she wasn't convinced. I explained I hadn't got a sick note because mine is a long standing condition, so I'd suffered in silence rather than bother my poor overworked GP. But she obviously doesn't share my concern for our ailing NHS.

'Your time-keeping's awful,' she said, 'and you've had two warnings already. I'm aware you have some social problems – but we are a business, not a welfare agency.'

And with that she handed me my P45.

So that's another place I'll never dare enter again. No more Marks and Sparks meals-for-one or discount knickers for me!

I feel desperate, Jean. I've no job, Marks won't give me a reference, I'm a thief and the last of my money has gone.

What can I do?

Please write to me, post haste.

Whatever that is.

With much love, your Juvenile Delinquent Victim-Of-Society friend.

(Maxine)

Dearest Jean,

Thank you from the bottom of my heart for sending me that tenner. I vowed to send it straight back, then realised I'd spent it. But I'll pay you back soon, I promise.

Half of it went in a plain brown envelope through the pizza place's door at 7.45 this morning. Dominic says robbing from a big company is just Redistributing Wealth, it isn't bad like nicking from a corner shop. But I know that nice till girl will have got into trouble over me. So I included a note about how my epilepsy sometimes suddenly rights itself but leaves me all forgetful. Now she'll know she was right to believe in me.

Besides, Dominic's not one to talk about what you can get away with. He's spent more time behind bars than in them — and that's saying something.

He is sweet though, even if he *is* out to lunch. Tonight, after I'd worn out my trainers tramping round all day to every shop for miles, begging for work, I ended up crying all over him. I even confessed that I'm now a hardened criminal too. He mopped my face with a painting rag, let me share his tomato soup and told me I should sign on for unemployment benefit. 'Let's get the state to take care of you,' he said.

I felt bad about becoming one of the *Sun*'s work-shy scroungers, but Dominic pointed out that I'll pay it all back one day in taxes, so really it's just a loan.

And how can I afford pride, when I'm down to my last Ryvita?

112

So I'm off there tomorrow.
Pray for me.
                    With much love, and ta again,

                    Maxie

                                    Cubicle One
                                The Benefits Barracks
                                    27 Whitehorn Rd
                                        London N7

                                        August 13th

Dear Jean,

I am now officially one of The Unemployed and
reduced to being a statistic.

Well, I would be, if the rotten government had allowed
me to sign on.

Today was a *disaster*. Dominic walked me to the signing
on office, but even though I felt dead nervous he
wouldn't come in with me. He was scared the Child
Support Agency detectives would think I was his daughter and start chasing him for fourteen years' worth of
overdue maintenance.

Once upon a time I would have been 100% embarrassed to be seen in a place like that. But now I'm on
the Ryvita Line I was only 90% embarrassed. After queu-
ing in the street for an hour, I even stopped facing the
wall.

Inside was *disgusting*. Filthy and cheerless. There's obviously a government planning department devoted to making dole offices horrible. Why paint any room bog brown and gruesome green? There was litter and fag ash everywhere and dried kiddy sick over the rock hard plastic chairs.

There aren't even enough chairs, so me and loads of other people waiting had to stand. When I did finally get to talk to an official, she was behind a thick glass screen, so I could only make myself heard by shouting.

It was *so* humiliating. I told the woman I'd queued two hours and was down to my best friend's last three quid. But all she did was laugh and tell me I couldn't 'sign on' until I'd registered in another building as unemployed.

This other place wasn't so bad. One section even had carpets and soft chairs, marked 'Professional and Executive Recruitment'. Naturally I went in there, seeing as one day I'll be a Professional, but when the interviewer asked about my last job and I said Marks bras she packed me off to another fag-ash place for Plebs.

When the next interviewer finally called me, she said I wasn't even *eligible* for unemployment benefit. I explained I was only 16 and had eaten my last Ryvita. Also that I desperately needed work or benefits so I could do my A Levels. That blew it totally.

'If you're studying,' she smirked, 'you're not available for work so you can't claim unemployment benefit. Next, please!'

I hung on in.

'I've done loads of GCSEs,' I protested. 'If my family could afford to keep me at school I could get to university. I could be the next Einstein for all you know.'

She threatened to call a security guard.

I just don't understand it. If I got to 18 and college,

then I could get an education grant. But there's nothing, it seems, to help you stay on that far.

Dad's right. The whole system is against people like me. And him. Yes, I'm even feeling sorry for him now. I saw him, you see: he was being interviewed himself, about whether he is genuinely looking for work.

I was leaving the dole office when I heard this voice that sounded like Dad. So I poked my head round the interview cubicle and saw this man slumped there, his shoulders all rounded and defeated. At first I thought, No, that can't be my dad, he's too *old*. But it *was* him, Jean, so despite my worst intentions I waited for him outside.

When he came out he looked all grey and creased and somehow done in. He didn't even think till we'd been chatting for a few minutes to ask why *I* was there. I said it was my half-day and I'd only come to keep a flatmate company. And Dad, who can usually sniff one of my whoppers a mile off, didn't even blink – he was that far gone.

Frankly I'd have felt better if he'd shouted and given me one of his lectures. But he didn't seem to care about anything. He'd just been told that, unless he gets a job within the month, they'll force him on to some retraining scheme.

'They wouldn't even say what kind,' he sighed. 'I could end up in an abattoir cutting up carcasses with Mad Cow Disease. And with no job at the end of it. These training placements are just excuses to get cheap labour. But if I say "No", I'll lose the miserable few quid they give me every week.'

Then he told me what they paid him and I was shocked. I hadn't realised how little it was. Oh, him and Mum have always gone on about how hard up they are, blah endless blah, but I'd never really understood exactly what that *meant*.

I wanted Dad to realise how Mature I've become, so I told him this when we went for a cuppa. I felt really close to him, just like in the old days – like we were two old comrades sharing our woes in a hostile world.

Except that I didn't share mine, of course – I didn't want to add to his grief by letting on how far I'd slipped from my original grand plan. I even told him Marks had made me a holiday relief supervisor.

I just wanted to cheer him up.

The trouble is, it worked too well.

'I knew my Maxi Taxi would shape up,' he said. 'That's my girl! Your mum's been fretting about you something awful.' He was obviously chuffed. He hasn't used that vomit–inducing nickname for me since I was about nine. It made me want to cry.

Then he patted my hand and said if I'd settled down to the idea of working at Marks, he and Mum would love to have me back.

'You've made your point, love – you've proved you're sensible. Now come back home where you belong.'

Jean, I can't tell you how attractive that sounded! Going home to a warm house, with dinners and telly and a phone, and parents who (sort of) love me! But how could I admit there wasn't an argument about school versus Marks anymore – because even Marks wouldn't have me?

I said thanks, I'd think about it, and yes, I would go round for Sunday dinner. And then off I limped, with nothing in the world except the quid Dad gave me.

I didn't want to take it but he insisted. Well, a man on the dole's got to be allowed his pride, hasn't he?

Should I own up to M & D? What do you think, Jean? Please write asap.

Your ever grateful friend,

Maxi Taxi

Dearest Jean,

Frankie is back! My one and only love! Begorrah, I hadn't realised how much I'd missed him until he staggered up the stairs this morning with his wonderful present, a sack of potatoes from his granny's farm.

I fell into his arms and the potatoes fell down the stairs but they still tasted like caviare after Frankie caught, boiled and buttered them. He even fried up some home-cured bacon from his granny's pigs. He said I looked a scrawny little thing and I said it's true, the way to a woman's heart is through her tum. We were dead romantic.

Then Frankie scooted off to enroll his beloved Deirdre in a bike maintenance workshop and Imelda came round. I realised I'd really missed her too, even if her clothes are seriously uncool. She offered to come round job hunting with me, and I said as long as she changed out of her combat gear first I'd be really grateful.

We were walking back to her place to dig out a dress from her pre-Catholic Guerilla stage when we passed this caff with a Help Wanted card in the window. Talk about the luck of the Irish − I was taken on!

117

The man said Honesty was more important than Experience, so it was fine when I explained that I had no references because I'd never had a job before. He was so desperate he let me start straightaway, mashing potatoes.

Mike's Caff is a *real* old, dirty greasy spoon. It even makes Bert's look respectable. Bits of plaster kept crumbling from the ceiling, so I was never sure if I was mashing potatoes or old paint. But Mike is friendly and the pay's better than nothing.

By knock-off time I knew what Mum meant about slaving all day over a hot stove! After I'd washed up my ninetieth cup it hit me that maybe Mum doesn't really have a second job at Bert's as a hobby.

I think I'd better apologise to her about that some time.

The Maloneys have obviously been plotting to Get Me Organised. Frankie turned up when I was leaving work and dragged me straight off to this Centre for the Unemployed he's found. I said it was too late, I was sorted now. But it was where he'd taken Deirdre for her face-lift today and he'd discovered it runs girls' advice sessions too.

He parked me with this terrifying woman who looked like a man, all crew cut and bovver boots with a ring through her nose. She gave him a dirty look because he called me a girl — apparently that's sexist, I'm really a Young Woman — and told him to wait outside. But when I told her my woes she was dead nice and suggested I do my As at a further education college. She said it's not like school, half the students are mums or workers on day release, so I wouldn't have to go in every day. I could still work and earn some money.

I asked if I'd get a college scarf to flaunt at the likes of

Muck Mouth Michelle still stuck in a stupid school uniform. She didn't know. Otherwise, she was really helpful.

I still can't manage the rent on part-time earnings so she suggested I try to make it up with M & D. That's what gave me my Inspiration. I was moseying around this centre afterwards and it's got groups for everything, motorbikes, single mums, single mums on motorbikes, the lot. I thought Dad might not be so cross with me for getting the sack and becoming a thief and still wanting to study and little things like that if I sorted out his life for him the way Frankie and Imelda are helping sort out mine. So I found the bloke who runs the Unemployed Group and asked him to give Dad a job.

He laughed and said that he would if he could, but the group's just a voluntary one to stop the unemployed feeling miserable. I said that made Dad their perfect candidate. I explained all about how he had been a shop steward and was dead good at organising things, but now that unemployment has broken up our happy home and he doesn't even have me to get militant over he feels no use to man or beast. I really sang his praises. The bloke said he was sure Dad would be a great help to them.

I'll tell Dad tomorrow at dinner about my fab reference.

Gotta run now. Frankie's taking me for a drink.

I'm a Friday Night Girl again!

Lotsa luv,

Maxine, your ultra cool college friend

PS   Make that Friday Night Young Woman.

Dearest Jean,

I can't sleep so here's a PPS.

I'm all muddled. Tonight I asked Frankie in for coffee after the pub and he gave me a funny look and said he had to be up early for work. Anyway, he doesn't drink coffee.

It was only after he'd gone that I realised he thought I was planning to Lead Him into Temptation. As if I would. After the fiasco with Suzy's boyfriend, I've learned my lesson.

I just didn't feel ready to let him go and be on my own again, counting the cracks in the bed-sit's walls.

Talking of Wicked Wayne, I could have died tonight, because he turned up at the Three Brewers. Frankie was busy working himself up to a big emotional speech about how he'd missed me when that B came in — with yet another girl from Marks on his arm.

I felt like the original Scarlet Woman because that sexist oik kept smirking at me and I was terrified he'd come up and make some nasty crack. Frankie got all uptight about the way he was looking at me and was all for Sorting Him Out. I felt dead swoony at the idea of my fella fighting over me. Then I remembered I'm a feminist as well as a pacifist so I made him put down the beer glass he was gripping and I threw it at Wayne instead.

Well, sort of accidentally on purpose tripped over him when I was passing, I mean. The beer went all down his trousers, which I thought was poetic justice. He looked annoyed but I wasn't even scared. I just started humming, 'Hitler only had one ball,' and hissed, 'One word out of

120

you, matey, and I'll tell everyone why this song reminds me of you!'

He went white as a sheet.

I felt really good afterwards, like I'd cut him down to size, so to speak.

The only thing is, I still haven't confessed to Frankie. And now I'm feeling really guilty. About Wayne; and Cas; and Frankie – for ever doubting him. He's so good to me, and it's not his fault he's no good at writing letters or that he's so dutiful he spent his summer helping his family instead of me.

He got quite choked telling me about his granny and all his childhood holidays on her little farm and how much she meant to him. I'd never even thought of that when I was wolfing down her potatoes.

I'm a selfish cow, Jean.

You've said that before when I've ignored the worries and questions in your letters and only talked about me. So I've carefully re-read your last three and here's my advice:

1) Ditch that hunky tanned Australian. He might seem the most glamorous male ever to hit The Whippet's Welcome, but that's only because you're grounded there. In a week's time you'll be free again to explore the cream of Ashton's manhood.

Anyway, when he's finished visiting his aunt and goes home you'll be broken-hearted. Plus, if you marry him and go to Australia I'll never see you again.

2) Even if you fail your GCSEs and are a barmaid for life I'll still be your friend, honest. Intellectuals need contact with people from all walks of life, even the humble ones.

3) I'm so sorry I've taken so long to send back your

121

best jumper that you left here. Either I didn't have the postage or the money for the launderette.

Of course I haven't been wearing it, but do you mind if I hang on to it until I've got through my college interview on Monday?

Thanks a million. It's because you're so understanding that you're my best friend.

With much love,

Max

PPPS   Please find enclosed a fiver from my pay towards the National Debt.

xxxx

and ta again.

August 21st

Dearest Jean,

Got your letter yesterday. Don't me daft, how could I have forgotten that our exam results are due? I'm counting the minutes till they're released.

I popped round to Mum and Dad's last night and casually reminded them. I kept mentioning Rosie's results party and how kind and concerned her parents are. But soppy Sue kept changing the subject back to *her* parties – her hen one, Derek's stag night, and their wedding buffet. Self, self, self, that's all that girl ever thinks about.

122

She's even taken over *my* half of OUR room for laying out her presents. MY BED was piled high with toasters, crockery, new sheets and three-legged knickers donated by Derek's laugh-a-minute mates. She took me upstairs for a guided tour of her gifts and her guesstimate, to the last p, of how much everything cost.

I didn't know whether to giggle or vomit. She's circled the whole lot with a huge sateen bow she's made, and every day she blasts her precious prezzie pile with air freshener.

Her excuse for this gross materialism is that it's customary for a bride to display her gifts. To me that sounds suspiciously like blackmail: give me something expensive or I'll show up your egg-timer in front of everyone.

My egg-timer wasn't even on display. I was quite hurt really.

Talking of marriage, I'm sorry I jumped the gun and assumed you'd want to marry your Aussie hunk. You're quite right, as 16-year-old geniuses-in-the-making we have better things to aim for.

I have taken your latest sensible advice. I was dying last night to tell M & D about my new educational Grand Plan. But I'll wait until the results are in and the wrinklies are (touch wood) impressed.

I've nearly sorted out college! On Monday I went to the one recommended by the nose ring lady and it was really exciting. The students have even got their own café, with potted palms instead of bossy dinner ladies. So I had a cuppa and pretended to read the T S Eliot book I'd brought for show.

It worked, no one saw through me and threw me out. It was dead scary, being around all those Mature Students – fellas as well, which will make a nice change from

Haringey's Horrid Girls High. But I looked the part OK. Your jumper with the Yin Yang motif really helped.

Of course I'm not intending to 'bung' your best jumper in a washing machine before returning it. Whatever made you think that? Now I'm living independently I know all about proper clothes care.

In return for me washing up last night, my mum's hand washing it.

Anyway, eventually I found the college admin lady and she was dead sympathetic when I explained about being a deprived child. She gave me the run-down on how to apply for a place and it looks like I'll make it as long as my results are half-way decent.

I've just had a horrible thought. What if, after all this careful planning, I prove my parents right – and FAIL?!!!

I can't face a life-time digging the plaster out of the mash in Mike's Caff.

I'm being daft. So are you. Of course we won't fail.

But I know what you mean about running out of nails to bite.

I've started on my toes . . .

Yours in nervous sisterhood,

Maxine the Nail-less

August 22nd

Dearest Fellow Genius Jean,

I've passed! All of them! Even biology, with my one sad diagram of a hydra doing a somersault! I got the lowest possible grade, but I still *passed*. And my other grades were great!

I know you won't mind me boasting, given you're now a recognised child prodigy too. It was really good of you to ring M & D and leave your results for me. I wouldn't have felt right whooping it up if you weren't.

Wasn't the waiting *awful*? The results were posted to my official address – M and D's – and I kept ringing them but the line was engaged. I was working at the caff all day and thought I'd have to wait till knock–off time to go round and be put out of my misery. Then who should walk into Mike's but Dad, brandishing that beautiful brown envelope with a great big silly grin!

He and Mum had opened it, of course, and then spent half the morning ringing their friends with the good news and trying to track me down. Dad had gone straight round to Marks you see, and practically had kittens when they said I didn't work there anymore.

'I felt so ashamed, Max, you only 16 and I didn't even know how you were making your living.'

I couldn't believe it. Humility from Attila the Hun?!? He even took my side when I explained I'd been sacked for trying to organise a trade union. Well, he said, what can you expect from a firm that keeps the royals in knickers.

Mike at the caff was great. He said I could have half an hour off to celebrate with my dad and even offered us a slap–up meal on the house. Dad was all for having it until I whispered to him about the side-servings of plaster. So he said Ta, mate, but we'll just have tea and a couple of plates. Then he whipped this tin out of a plastic bag and produced the saddest, sweetest cake you've ever seen.

Do you remember how hit and miss my mum's cakes

are? Well, this was her floppiest, messiest jam sponge *ever*. But knowing that she'd sweated over it before rushing off to sweat all day at Bert's made me want to cry.

Even Dad had done his bit. He'd run down the road to Mr Habib's and bought a bag of M&M's to write Well Done Maxie! on top.

He'd tracked me down through the flat and Dominic.

'There was this right weird geezer at your gaff. He kept going on about how he had a lovely long-lost daughter too.'

I guess being lectured by Dom on how precious I am, and seeing my 'gaff' in the cold light of day, must have really shamed Dad, because suddenly he came over all sentimental. He even gripped my hand and begged my forgiveness. Well, what he actually said was, 'I don't always get it right, do I?' which is the nearest he'll ever get. It was good enough for me and set me off and made my mascara run.

Then I had to get back to slaving over Mike's mash. But I promised Dad I'd come home tomorrow for a celebration tea. Well, it's Rosie's party tonight. Besides, if Mum and Dad are suddenly my devoted fans, it's good tactics playing hard to get. After they've had a night's kip and the shock of giving birth to a genius has sunk in, they'll probably *beg* me not to throw away my life peeling potatos and picking out plaster in a greasy spoon.

Gorra run. I've only got a mingy hour to get ready. Plus Her Highness has invited me in for a celebratory sherry and I'll end up having to tally up all her tins. She's insisted I do it every week since I told her about my talent for stock-taking at Marks. Watch out, Muck Mouth Michelle, here comes the working class's Glamm-iest Genius!

(Excepting you, of course.)

126

WELL DONE TO YOU, TOO!
Oodles of love, relief, joy, pride, glorious etcetera,

The most Mentally Magnificent Max
(also known as 'Modest Maxine')

xxxxxxxxxxxxxxxxxxx

A Tipsy PS After the Party

Dear Jean,

I can't work out how I managed to get addled at
Rosie's. Her mum made a huge bowl of fruit punch and
there were so many girls dissolving it with their tears I
was sure it was alcohol-free. That's why I had eight
glasses.

Excuse the wonky writing but you'll be so proud of
the mature way I ended my five-year association with
Muck Mouth Michelle.

Naturally those of us who were crying for joy were
tactful about her stupidity. She got two pathetic passes.
None the less she swanned in in this flash new coat and
asked if *my* parents had bought me a suitable GCSE
present, like a copy of the *Big Issue*, perhaps. Ha bloomin'
ha. I resisted bitching back because I knew deep down
she was vulnerable. Finally, after a few glasses, she showed
it and started snivelling.

I looked at her, remembering how often she had
laughed at me for needing free school meals, and
momentarily felt torn between rubbing her face in it

127

and displaying Christian charity. Naturally my wiser impulse won. I offered her a tissue and said she couldn't help being a moron.

I'm not sure if it was then, or when I pointed out that she was probably still qualified to *clean* a doctor's surgery, that she hit me.

I had to defend myself and it was turning into a major scrap until Rosie's dad pulled us apart. He gave me a lecture in the kitchen, about success being the best revenge and not bearing grudges. I agreed and asked for a prawn cocktail to prove how sophisticated I was. Then I sneaked off with it into the hall, tore open a couple of stitches in the hem of Muck Mouth's lovely new coat and slipped in the prawns.

Cop a whiff of those in a week's time, Michelle!

Two were from you, for all those times she taunted you about your nose. That's one for each nostril.

Your loyal friend,

Max The Mature

Somewhere in North London

August 23rd

Now read on . . .

Dearest Jean,

My celebration tea at home tonight was great. When I saw the roast potatoes and gravy I knew I was home and dry – Mum had done a proper Sunday dinner and Dad had even splashed out on a bottle of wine, which we only *ever* have at Christmas.

Stingy Sue actually gave me A PRESENT! (A spare set of toasters from her wedding pile.) And M & D gave me a gold charm bracelet with the initial M in case I ever forget my name even though I'm now officially a genius. It's naff but kind of sweet. Just like them, really.

Then Mum had a second glass of Blue Nun and cried into it. She even said Fine to college as long as I work at the caff a couple of days a week, to help support myself. 'Your dad and I will manage somehow,' she said, 'without letting you go short.' And that set me off blubbing too and I promised they'd never regret it and that when I'm rich and famous I won't put them in an old people's home.

Then to cap it all, they produced tickets for the drama group's opening show. Amanda had flogged 'em to Mum when she'd caught her hanging out her washing. It's at the Unemployed Centre and Dad's molten because the mean old cow didn't even allow him the usual discount for UB40s.

I'd have preferred to join Sue at her boring wedding rehearsal, now that I've grown out of Performance Art. But as Mum and Dad have never before shown much interest in what interests me, I was really touched. Besides, I thought I should go along just to show Cas etc. there's no hard feelings, and ya boo sucks why would I want to be in their lousy group when I've just pulled off a bunch of GCSEs?

I loved the show because it was so *bad*. The acting, the dancing, *everything*. No wonder I hated rehearsals. That proves I'm a True Artiste. I must have known all along it was rubbish.

129

I didn't dare look at Mum and Dad in case they were cross I'd ever wasted my time on this. Then I heard this strange snorting sound and turned round to find that Dad had stuffed his hanky in his mouth, to stop himself from laughing!

It was Cas's big poetic number as the Talking Foetus that finally finished us off. Jolyon the Midwife squirted some tomato sauce over him and then he crawled across the stage in his body stocking and intoned:

> The young are expelled from the womb
> Like a coffin from a tomb
> For the homeless there is no room
> The Tories bring only doom
> Let us sweep them away with a broom.

Well, Dad exploded fit to bust and the hanky shot out of his mouth on to the head of the man in front. There was this kind of hushed silence and then everyone in the audience was belly laughing too.

Mum and me bundled Dad out. While he was recovering outside that nice bloke from the Unemployed Group came by to see what all the noise was about. I told him Dad was the really miserable man I'd told him about, which set Dad off laughing again. I thought that'd ruin his chances of qualifying for the group but it turned out he and this bloke Bob knew each other from some shop stewards' committee, and next thing they were slapping each other on the back and Dad was slagging off the poncey middle classes just like in the good old days.

Me and Mum went off to raid the refreshment stall, and after she'd endured some camomile tea (the only kind available) we found Dad and his old mate planning a whole new future for the centre. Bob said it could really do with a proper militant like Dad, to prevent its takeover by the hanging-basket brigade; and if he could control the young tearaways in the bike maintenance group, it might even lead to a job.

Well fancy that! My dad a *social worker*!

When we got him home, Mum and me gave him a good ribbing about turning into a Do-Gooder but he was all cheerful at the thought of having something to do and for the first time in months I remembered that I love him.

Then Dad said, 'It's a bit late for you to be going back to that bed-sit, Max. Why don't you stay over with us?' Mum was nodding furiously. 'Yes, for as long as you like, love.'

Nobody exactly said, 'Please forgive us, Darling, and come home,' but I knew that's what they meant. So when Mum offered to make me hot chocolate and run a bath for me I accepted graciously. I even allowed her to fill my hottie, even though it's August.

I didn't let on I cried in the bath, and again when I found that Sue had cleared her presents off my bed and written me a sweet note, 'Welcome back, horrid little sister'. But I was a bit puffy eyed when Mum turned up to tuck me in like I was little again, and maybe she guessed. She kissed me and said we'd get my things tomorrow, as though we'd already discussed it all and agreed, and suddenly I was boo-hooing in her arms and telling her how horrid it had been and how I'd never again call her a cow for being too tired after work to iron my clothes and now I knew what housework involved I hadn't even wiped up the water on the bathroom floor with clean towels.

'I used my clothes,' I joked, 'like you're supposed to.'

Then she started crying too and said she and Dad were

131

so sorry they hadn't believed in me, it was just that no one in our family had ever passed anything before and things had been so tight.

Just when I thought I couldn't cry any more she said, 'Oh, I nearly forgot – Frankie left this for you earlier,' and produced some crumpled, oil-stained tissue paper from her pocket. It contained a golden key to add to my bracelet and a little card, 'To Max, because the future's all yours and you're so bright and brave.'

He'd forgotten to add 'beautiful' but if I ever call him Frigid Frankie again, *please* will you bash me over the head?

SEE YOU NEXT WEEK AT SUE'S WEDDING!

Meanwhile, here's the last fiver I owe you. Don't waste it on Sue, save it for a treat for when you too go back to boring old studying.

I know I'm not a Catholic any more, well I never even became one, but tonight I said a long prayer of thanks. It's mean me only talking to God when I'm desperate, like if I've got zits just before a party. I've got so much to thank Him for.

And you, the cleverest part-time barmaid in Ashton-under-Lyne. For sticking by me.

Yours, cuddling up to my Care Bears nightcase,
With much love from your best friend,

Maxine,

future star of 'Home in Hornsey'

132

Some of this book was inspired by own experiences: I
first left home at 16. It was rarely funny, it was frightening
and lonely, and I'd recommend any young person in need
to get good advice before taking such a drastic step.

I guess I partly wrote this book because laughter heals.

But after writing the first draft, I did something quite
strange. I shoved the manuscript in a drawer, devoted the
next few years to journalistic investigation of cruelty to
children in care, and told The Women's Press I had
nothing to show them beyond the opening pages and a
few notes.

I genuinely forgot I had written this book: it was an
'unfinished' project I felt too busy to complete. Certainly
I was busy: it took dozens of newspaper articles before
our exposés of the appalling conditions in Islington's
children's homes were believed. But finally we got somewhere. Government inquiries were ordered, heads rolled,
reforms were introduced, and a few kids' chances of
survival were improved.

At last I had time again for Maxine. I dug out my
'notes', and found to my amazement I'd already written
French Leave – from beginning to end. I'd already rescued
Maxine, and she still made me laugh.

I quickly completed a final draft.

I don't know what this means, except maybe I needed
a victory in the real world of children who have no
secure homes or families to turn to, before I could allow
myself to go back to the fictional one I created. Because
in my campaigning I was fighting too for me, and the
young person I once was.

Today life is even harder for teenagers from troubled

backgrounds. And getting help can be very hard. Sometimes you can't get through on a helpline, or an official is rude, or a person in a position of trust turns out to be untrustworthy.

But I genuinely believe more people in this world are good than bad. So if you need help of any kind – please keep trying. And keep believing in yourself.

grab a livewire!

real life, real issues, real books, real bite

Rebellion, rows, love and sex... pushy boyfriends, fussy parents, infuriating brothers and pests of sisters... body image, trust, fear and hope... homelessness, bereavement, friends and foes... raves and parties, teachers and bullies... identity, culture clash, tension and fun... abuse, alcoholism, cults and survival... fat thighs, hairy legs, hassle and angst... music, black issues, media and politics... animal rights, environment, veggies and travel... taking risks, standing up, shouting loud and breaking out...

...grab a Livewire!

For a free copy of our latest catalogue,
send a stamped addressed envelope to:

The Sales Department
Livewire Books
The Women's Press Ltd
34 Great Sutton Street
London EC1V 0DX
Tel: 0171 251 3007
Fax: 0171 608 1938